Zombie Diaries

Fall Semester Senior Year

The Mavis Saga

By
R.W.K. Clark

Edition 1

United States Copyright Office
#1-6140530816
Library of Congress Control Number: 2017907165
International Standard Book Numbers
ISBN-10: 1948312042
ISBN-13:978-1948312042
ASIN: B07HJ9Q5BT

/200801

ZOMBIE DIARIES SERIES

Zombie Diaries - Homecoming Junior Year - ZD1
ISBN-10: 0997876778 ISBN-13: 978-0997876772

Zombie Diaries - Winter Formal Junior Year - ZD2
ISBN-10: 0997876786 ISBN-13: 978-0997876789

Zombie Diaries - Prom Junior Year - ZD3
ISBN-10: 0997876794 ISBN-13: 978-0997876796

Zombie Diaries - Summer Break Junior Year - ZD4
ISBN-10: 1948312034 ISBN-13: 978-1948312035

Zombie Diaries - Fall Semester Senior Year - ZD5
ISBN-10: 1948312042 ISBN-13: 978-1948312042

Zombie Diaries - Senior Graduation - ZD6
ISBN-10: 1948312050 ISBN-13: 978-1948312059

CONTENTS

ACKNOWLEDGMENTS

I dedicate this novel to my wonderful readers and for all the amazing people I've met and those I haven't. To my family and loved ones, all your support will not be forgotten.

This book was made possible by reviews from readers like you.

Thank you

R.W.K. Clark

CHAPTER 1

The girl stood at the door of the house, holding it open with one hand and toting a suitcase in the other, purse hanging over her shoulder by the strap. With a smile, she took one last look around the massive living space, satisfied with what she saw. She couldn't have been happier, or fuller if she tried.

The bodies of the man and woman, or what was left of them, were strewn about everywhere in the room. Blood pooled here and there on the marble floor, bones were scattered, and a few shreds of flesh hung randomly from various items in the room. Her smile grew; it was the most beautiful thing she had ever seen! Unfortunately, she couldn't stay to appreciate her masterpiece. It was time to get to the airport and catch her flight. With a loud burp, she left the house, making sure to close and lock the door behind her.

As she walked to the car, her mind ticked off the items in her purse, she had all she needed. Her passport and countless credit cards were all taken from the people lying dead on the floor. She was perfectly well-equipped, and it was time to return to the place from where she came. Her airline ticket was waiting for her, and her flight would be leaving in just four hours. Excited, she thought about seeing her friend again; oh, the girl would be blown away! There were plans made for her friend… plans to keep and make her one of her own. Together, they would get back at everyone who ever gave them a hassle in that crummy town. She couldn't wait to set the plan into action.

But there was one person in her mind that caused rage to build when she thought of her. That person had been the cause of all this, had been the one to rip her life apart. Not that she really cared anymore; she loved the way things were now, and she wouldn't have it any other way. But instead of feeling a sense of gratefulness toward the person, she felt only hate. Once she got settled in and had her best friend by her side, the two of them would pay this person a visit, and they would make her pay, satisfying that hatred once and for all.

After that, she would get on with doing exactly what she wanted to do, when she wanted to do it: eating fresh, yummy human flesh, all day, and every day.

Steering the car up the highway toward the airport, she flipped on the radio and began to hum to the tune pumping from the speakers, a hard rock number with foreign lyrics that she had never really come to understand, even though she had lived in Tuscany for months. The truth was, she hated Italy, but the Italians who lived there tasted wonderful.

As she drove, she couldn't help but wonder if the Americans she had been born and raised around would taste as good as her parents. "Buon appetito!"

CHAPTER 2

"Mavis! If you don't hurry up, you won't have time to eat, and you'll need your energy, today!"

Jane Harvey stood directly outside her daughter's bedroom door, which was locked tight so Mavis could finish cleaning up the last of the cow heart that Matt had provided for her the night before. She didn't know why her mother had to panic: she still had two hours before Matt would even come to pick her up for the first day of Senior Year. She had plenty of time to shower, eat, and even chat with her mom for a while.

"I'm getting ready to shower, Mom!" Mavis shouted through the door as she rolled up her garbage bag. "I have plenty of time, and you know me; I'm never late. I'll be out to eat in a bit."

Jane let out a sigh loud enough to be heard through the door. "Okay, then. I'll see you shortly."

Mavis couldn't help but smile as she finished cleaning up her mess. When she was finished, she threw on her bathrobe and made her way to the shower, humming as she went. Her mother was more excited about the first day of school than she was, and the thought of it tickled her to no end. It would be a big year, she could admit it, but Jane was simply beside herself. While Mavis washed up, she thanked her lucky stars for a mother that most kids her age would die to have.

∞

Forty-five minutes later, Mavis was settling in at the kitchen table. A plate loaded with everything from pancakes and hash browns to bacon and fried eggs sat before her. Even though she had just gorged herself on cow heart, she knew she could stuff in every last bite of the food. Her appetite knew no bounds, even though the food wouldn't be the least bit satisfying. It would make her mother happy to see her eat it all, and that was what mattered to Mavis.

"Looks amazing, Mother."

Picking up her fork, she dug right in while Jane topped off her coffee and took her own seat. The woman watched her daughter eat for a while, sipping her coffee, and smiling. Jane waited until Mavis got halfway through her food before starting to converse.

"Are you excited?" she asked, a twinkle in her eye. "The first day of Senior Year. Just think, Mav: college soon, then you'll be a career woman, with your entire future ahead of you."

Mavis nodded and swallowed her bite. "Yeah. A little nervous, too, I guess. Not about school, but about the fact that it is the last year. It seems like just yesterday I was a freshman, and now I'm going to be taking the SATs and applying to colleges." With a bite on the fork, part-way to her mouth, she gave her mom a serious look. "So, you and Dad are really okay with me going to Ohio U… I mean, okay with me staying so close to home and all?"

Jane snorted, signifying that Mavis was speaking the obvious. "Are you kidding?" she paused and caught herself, realizing that she wasn't that supportive of Mavis' future independence or that which was current, for that matter. "I mean, don't get me wrong, dear. You are free to pursue whatever avenue you desire, even if that means going out of state… or even further. But the fact that you will be close to home is a major relief to me, especially as a mother with only one daughter."

Mavis looked up at her and smiled. "I know, Mom, you don't have to explain. I feel fortunate that Ohio U has such an incredible child psychology program. It will really help me be the best I can be in my field."

For as long as she could remember, Mavis had wanted to work with kids. She'd focus especially on those who had been orphaned, or who had problems adapting because they were less fortunate in one way or another. She wasn't specifically sure about all of the exacts, but she knew that kids would be in the picture. When she had first gotten "ill," all of that had been threatened, at least in her mind. But now that she knew what she really was, and was learning to live with it properly. Her confidence was growing once again, and she was sure she would be able to continue on and pursue her original dream.

But the truth was, she didn't just choose Ohio U in Toledo because of its great child psych program, though it was one of the best programs of its kind in the nation. She also chose it because attending there would enable her to stay at home, and at the current time, she knew that was for the best. It wouldn't do to eat one of her dormmates just because she got too eager to be out on her own. Maybe by the end of the Senior Year, she would have something figured out with food, and she would be able to move out. But until then, it was best to take things slow. Both Mavis and Matt agreed that the next logical step, considering her condition, was to have her own apartment, and neither Jane nor Todd disagreed.

Mavis cleaned up the rest of her plate while Jane began to go on and on about what a great school Ohio U was like Mavis needed to be convinced. She patiently let her mother speak, nodding and "mm-hmm-ing" in all the right places, until she knew that it was time to get her things together so she could leave. Matt would be arriving in all of ten minutes, and with each passing second, Mavis felt her excitement growing. It had been a long summer, filled with all sorts of drama and doubt. But now she was heading into the Senior Year. It was a new beginning, a giant first step toward tomorrow, and it was getting ready to start.

As if on cue, the doorbell rang; Matt was early.

Jane jumped up and grabbed Mavis' plate off the table. "You'd better get that, honey. I'm sure it's Matthew."

But she was already half-way to the front door when Jane spoke. Grabbing the knob, she flung the door open with a beaming smile. Matt greeted her with the same.

"So," she said, "what do you think of my 'First Day of School' outfit?"

He looked her up and down, unfazed by the off-beat "hello" she gave him. One look at her black denim skirt, torn black leggings, black spaghetti strap top, and combat boots, and he gave her a nod of approval.

"Love it, babe. Am I just as acceptable?"

She didn't even give his attire a glance. Instead, Mavis threw her arms around him and planted a solid kiss on his lips. "Of course, you're always at your very hottest. Do you have any doubt?"

"Of course not." Matt spared an extra kiss on her cheek, then stepped back and gave her a more serious gaze. "So, how are you feeling about today? Confident in your personal strength? You have your vapor rub, right? No need to put yourself, or others, at risk."

Mavis nodded and gave a quick glance to the inside of her bag. "Check."

Her response drew a satisfied sigh from Matt. He put his hands on her shoulders and looked at her for a moment before drawing her to him in an affectionate embrace. Mavis moaned and hugged him back as best as she could for her arms were full. Matt laughed and let her go.

"Here, Mav," he said with a smile. "Let me take your stuff."

Before long, the pair was in Mavis' convertible, making their way to Westside High School.

CHAPTER 3

"So, are you nervous?"

Matt pulled the car out of the driveway and aimed it in the direction of the school. He had left his own vehicle at home and walked to Mavis' house so they could take her car, but she always let him drive anyway. It felt better to let someone else be in control when it came to some things.

She gave a shrug, her heart immediately dropping at his question. "Yeah. I guess I am, but not for the reasons my mother thinks. She thinks I'm nervous simply because it's Senior Year, but as I'm sure you know, there's a bit more to it than that."

He reached over with his right hand and gave her leg a pat. "I figured. Wanna talk about it before we get there?"

"I don't know," she replied. "I guess. I just feel weird knowing that most of the faculty will be different, thanks to… me. Have you stopped to think that you, me, Kim, and Shawn are some of the only original kids from last year left? I mean, the Senior Class is going to be really, really small this year. And all the new teachers? I mean, it's going to be so strange, and knowing it's all my fault doesn't help."

Mavis had good reason to be on edge about the first day of Senior Year. At Junior Prom, during the execution of a little prank she and Matt had planned, she had lost control and managed to consume most of the Junior Class, along with the faculty members who were chaperoning the event. The guilt Mavis carried around with her over the entire ordeal was more than she could express, and she barely had the energy as she thought about it to extend the effort.

"I guess... it's just that..."

Matt slowly pulled the car over and put the transmission into neutral. Turning to her, he studied her for a moment, giving her a bit more time to continue, if she chose, but she did not. After several seconds, he took her hand and stroked the back of it with his thumb.

"It's important that you forgive yourself, and that means facing the day." When Mavis said nothing in reply, he continued. "You know the entire incident was completely unintentional. I know there were several staff and students you cared about who are gone now. But you will build new relationships, and the year will go on. Do you think you are able to do it?"

Mavis nodded.

Matt turned back to the wheel and put the car into gear. "Good, because anything less will just raise suspicions and lead to trouble. We both must put one foot in front of the other and get on with life. You've learned a lot about your condition: things won't be the same this time."

"I know."

But as they drove, she couldn't get her mind off the truth: it was going to be like starting at a brand-new school. Miss Hawkins, her literature teacher and the one who had been her personal favorite, was dead and gone, as were several others. Most all of Westside's remaining students were grieving at one level or another, but she literally felt torn apart inside, for a couple of incomprehensible reasons. How could she face anyone? How could she look the students, old, surviving staff, or even a single new faculty member in the eye? She wasn't sure how she was going to do it, but she knew that she had to, for the sake of her family, for Matt, and for herself.

Mavis took a deep breath and said, "I know what has to be done, and I'm going to do it. It just seems to be easier said than done, you know what I mean?"

Matt nodded. "It's going to be fine."

Pulling into Westside's lot, he quickly found a space and parked the car. After shutting off the sedan, he then reached into the back seat for his own bag before turning to her once again. He gave her a wink and an air kiss.

"So, before we jump in head-first, what classes do you have again?" he asked.

Mavis reached into the front zipper pocket of her computer bag and withdrew her schedule. "Um, let's see… First period I have Advanced Composition with Duncan… that's a new teacher."

"Cool," Matt said. "I have that too, so we can walk together. What else?"

"Second is Health and Nutrition, third is a study hall."

Matt scanned his schedule. "Okay... I have Graphic Design I for second period, but we have that study hall together. For fourth, I have Computer Programming, and fifth is Quantitative Lit., then Journalism. Finally, I have a study hall again. Anything more in common?"

"Just the last study hall," Mavis replied. "At least we have two mellow periods together."

"Right." Matt tucked away his schedule, as did Mavis. "So, have you talked to Kim? Do you have anything with her?"

Mavis smirked a bit as she thought of her best friend since the first grade. In years past, the two of them would have been doing this together, but since Kim Coleman had started dating Shawn Maher last year, the pair had gotten pretty serious. Now Kim and Mavis mostly talked on the phone, and they only hung out now and then on the weekends and holidays. Kim was even discussing marriage after graduation, which made Mavis feel a bit melancholy; she was so glad to have Matt in her life to fill the void left by Kim's growing relationship.

"Well, you know Kim," she replied with a chuckle. "A couple of her subjects are still pre-requisites that she either blew off or got crappy grades in. I know she has French, and she has to do Trig again. The only class we have in common if I remember right is last period study hall."

Matt grinned and shook his head. "It'll be a seventh-period party, then! I'll have to hook up with Shawn and find out what he has, too." He paused and gave her a longer gaze, one that signified he wanted her full attention. "You know," he continued, once she turned her eyes to him, "I'm nervous too if it makes you feel any better. I mean, I know I wasn't here for any more than half a year, but knowing what happened at prom makes me wonder how many of the new teachers had to really be coaxed… hard. They have to be a bit nervous, too. I'm sure some of them are temps or subs, just filling in until more permanent teachers are hired. I guess what I'm trying to say is that I feel bad for them too. You know what I mean?"

A sad look came over Mavis' face, and she could do nothing more than nod.

"So, I just wanted to tell you that I really think all of us, everyone, is in this together today." Matt reached out and gave her hand a gentle squeeze.

Fighting back the tears of guilt and remorse, Mavis replied. "Yeah… I've thought of that already. We just all need to be easy on each other, students and teachers alike. I know I will be… especially me."

Leaning over to give her a final kiss, Matt squeezed her hand one last time, and the two of them got out of the car and headed toward the school building, holding hands for dear life.

They weren't halfway across the lot when they were suddenly approached by Kim Coleman and Shawn

Maher.

"Hey! We couldn't have had more perfect timing, right?"

Kim was her typical bubbly self, while Shawn stood on the sidelines with a somewhat dim smile on his face. He looked excited, but he had always been just a few light bulbs short of a four-pack, so he was typically quiet like this at the beginning of all greetings and conversations. Shawn was a jock, through and through; it was best to be patient with him when it came to social interactions.

All four stopped and stood in a circle. "Yeah, good timing," Mavis said, her smile plastic, but existent. "How do you feel about today, Kim? I mean, knowing all you know…"

Kim studied her friend briefly, then offered her a soft smile and understanding eyes. "It was what it was, and today is what it is." She reached out and stroked Mavis' arm softly. "And what it is, is a new beginning. You are going to love Senior Year, all of us are. Before you know it, Girl, junior year is going to be a faded memory with nothing more than a few sharp edges."

"Hear, hear!" Matt couldn't resist but offer his two cents of support, and Mavis couldn't help but smile.

With a deep breath, she replied, "Well, I'm ready if all of you are. I can't tell you how much all of your support and trust means to me."

Kim spoke up, a mischievous smile on her face. "You have taken precautions, right? I don't want lunch to be my last class if you know what I mean!"

"Very funny, Kim." Mavis tried to be stern with her friend, but she couldn't stop the smile that broke out on her face at Kim's amusing words. Well, it was best to make the best of the situation, and appropriate laughter was good for the soul.

After another deep breath, Mavis took the hands of both Matt and Kim, who in turn took Shawn's. "Let's do this thing, shall we?"

So, in a row, with beaming smiles and clasped hands, the four friends made their way toward the main entrance of Westside High to face the tension-filled first day of their Senior Year.

R.W.K. Clark

CHAPTER 4

"I think it's just what I'm looking for. How much is required to sign the lease?"

Shanice Hall was looking at the realtor lady without flinching or smiling. The older, gray-haired woman had acted just a tad suspicious when they had met the first two times, but once Shanice secured a home loan under the name Aneta Hall for the full listing price, the woman's attitude had changed dramatically.

"As you know," she continued. "I have the funds available to you. I am interested only in moving in as soon as possible."

Mrs. Keister, the realtor, gave Shanice a syrupy smile that didn't touch her eyes. "Of course, Mrs. Hall; all is a go. I just want to be sure this is truly the type of home you are looking for before we take care of all the red tape."

Shanice gave an appeasing smile and cast another slow glance around the place. Two-bedroom loft apartment, minimal light, mostly wood, which was easy enough to cover and keep clean. Spacious enough for all her dining indulgences, and since it was the only unit that would be occupied on this side of the condominium building, it would provide her with the privacy she needed.

"Do you want to sell it to me or not?"

Mrs. Keister changed her apprehensive demeanor like she had flipped a switch. "Of course. We just have the paperwork to sign over here. I have the escrow check, and since the residence is available for immediate occupancy, I have the keys for you as well. I just thought that you may want something a bit more… luxurious. You and your husband had always leaned that way in the past."

The women walked over to a folding card table that Mrs. Keister was using to do business. A stack of paperwork was ready for Shanice to sign, under her mother's name, of course. For a split second, as she sat to read and sign the paperwork, she thought of how thankful she was that she was pretty much a clone of her mother, Aneta. She had been using her identification and financials since arriving back in the states, and it had been going as smoothly as cream poured over strawberries. All she had to do was tell the realtors and their companies that her husband, Michael, was staying behind in Tuscany for an undetermined amount of time to finish providing care to his most desperate of patients. Only Mrs. Keister had shown apprehension. On their first meeting, the woman had shown no hesitation when it came to exhibiting her doubt about Shanice really being Aneta.

"My Lord, Aneta," the woman had gasped. "You look like you're twenty years younger. What have you been doing?"

Shanice had simply smiled, and in her standoffish way, replied, "It takes a lot of money to look like this, Harriet. I'll take your words, and your abrupt attitude, as a compliment. Now, do you mind showing me around the place?"

That had appeased the woman through the first two showings, but today, during the third and final showing, Harriet Keister was acting very strange, as if she had spent several waking nights trying to put her finger on what the difference was in Aneta Hall. Not just her youthful appearance… that could mean anything. But she just didn't seem to be the same person; she was harder, a bit more condescending, and had no interest in small talk or gossip. It was almost as if Harriet was speaking to an entirely different person, someone much more abrasive, more… sinister.

But, to Harriet Keister, money talked, and bullshit walked, and "Aneta" Hall had the money to fund her own marathon.

Both of them sat down and turned their attention to the extensive paperwork before them; they would be here another two hours, but that didn't matter to Shanice. All she was concerned about was getting the task completed and getting moved in. She didn't have many household needs, but she didn't care; she had enough money to fully stock the place. By the time she was done, it would appear to the visiting stranger that she had been there for years.

For the next long while, they completed all necessary

paperwork, which had been made easier by the fact that Shanice purchased the place for the full asking price. It seemed like forever, but before she knew it, Harriet Keister was handing her a folder with all of her necessary documents and dropping the keys into her hand. She stood up quickly, eyes darting here and there as if she wanted to make as rapid a departure as possible.

"Well, I must be going," the woman said lightly. "I hope Dr. Hall finds this to his liking, so let me know how it goes, Mrs. Hall."

Shanice inhaled deeply through her nose; she could smell the aroma of the middle-aged woman's skin, and while it was certainly tempting, it simply didn't reek of the freshness she so preferred in her younger entrees. It was this fact that had kept her from losing control and devouring the woman as soon as she walked in. Well, coupled with liberal smears of perfume under her nose. But now, the perfume was fading, and Harriet's scent was really starting to come through. The strange thing was that the woman seemed to "feel" that Shanice smelled her, and the fact that she wanted to leave as soon as possible couldn't be more obvious.

After a long moment and several apprehensive glances, Harriet Keister said, with a plastic, shaky smile on her face, "Unless you have any other questions, it looks like we're all finished here." She grabbed her purse from where it was hanging on the back of her chair, then began to stuff her file into her attaché case with trembling hands. "Be sure to let me know if you need anything, Mrs. Hall."

Shanice watched her, an amused smile on her face. How she would love to devour this plump woman who smelled like banana bread, but that wouldn't do at all; she had other plans that required her to demonstrate self-control, and now was the perfect time to do just that. Maybe another time, in a dark alley, or in the woman's living room, but not here, where her place would be all bloody before she even settled in.

"Yes, I'll be sure to do that, Mrs. Keister," Shanice replied. "By the way, what is that scent you are wearing?"

"Me?" The woman offered a nervous chuckle and a dismissive wave of her hand. "Just 'Vanilla Dream,' nothing expensive."

Shanice laughed. "Well, it smells absolutely... delicious."

She gave a lightning fast lick to her lips, which Mrs. Keister didn't miss. "Thanks again. I hope you enjoy your new home."

With that, the woman scurried out the door as though she was being chased by a rat, or spiders, or the like. Shanice watched her, entertained by the woman's insight, which seemed to have communicated clear danger to her and made her uncomfortable. Oh, well, now she was gone. It was time for Shanice to get some furniture, beverages, and maybe something nice and bloody to eat from the store. She needed something, anything, to tide her over until nightfall when she would be able to safely indulge her appetite the proper way.

After putting her new house keys on the keychain to the luxury sports car she had purchased, Shanice grabbed her purse and left the building. Her mind was ticking off the order in which she would run her errands. Without having to think about it too much, she made a mental note that she needed some more clothing and makeup; the flaking skin on her lower neck was becoming a bit more noticeable, and she wouldn't allow the gross condition to make her look like a walking dead person.

Humming, she made her way out to the luxury sports car and daydreamed about the day she would come face to face with her target, Mavis Harvey.

As she got into her car and started the engine, she thought about the salesman who had sold the vehicle to her. He certainly had smelled yummy, even for a sleazy car salesman, and now she thought about making him her next meal. It wasn't like she would have to deal with him directly in the future, after all, and he saw plenty of customers in a single day. The chances of his death coming back to her were slim to none. Yes, she would wait until just before the dealership closed, and she would follow him when he left work. The thought of sinking her teeth into his muscular torso made her mouth water pleasantly.

Pulling out of the small parking lot, Shanice began to hum once again.

CHAPTER 5

The first day of senior high was definitely uncomfortable, but not for the reasons Mavis would have thought. Also, it wasn't as bad as she had anticipated; it seemed like she was in an alternate reality, in a play she had starred in before, but with an entirely new cast. The worst thing about the day was all the sentiment and condolences the new teachers, and old ones seemed to think they should shower her with. Thankfully, she was easily able to demonstrate grace and thanks in her acceptance, and it made things go much more smoothly.

Her first class was Advanced Composition. Writing had always been one of her favorite pastimes, along with reading books, so this was one class she was particularly looking forward to. Last year, she had Miss Hawkins for creative writing, and she found herself wondering if Hawkins would have taught this class as well, had the woman survived Junior Prom, that is. Knowing that thinking about her old favorite teacher wouldn't help, so she focused on the things her new teacher, Mr. Duncan, had to say to introduce himself to the class, and the students to each other.

She was very unsure of the new educator, especially since he was instructing one of her favorite subjects. She wanted to keep her distance, but after introductions, Mr. Duncan told the class to engage in a brief essay of five-hundred words summarizing their lives and future goals. This would give him a type of individual gauge to judge their skill levels, as well as get to know each and every one of them on a more personal level.

Mavis finished the task quickly and efficiently, and a quick re-read told her the work was above satisfactory level. She decided to read a copy of *Out to Sea*, a piece she had just started the weekend before for no other reasons than she was bored and she had always wanted to read the book after having seen the movie. But just as she laid the copy on her desk and opened to her marked page, Mr. Duncan suddenly appeared right next to her.

"Mavis Harvey?" he whispered in her ear.

She jumped, then looked up at the man with wide eyes; had she already managed to get on his bad side somehow? Had she finished the elementary-level first-day assignment too soon for the man's taste?

"Yes, Mr. Duncan?"

A soft smile curved over his lips, and Mavis immediately recognized a soft look of pity and compassion in his eyes.

"May I have a private word with you for a moment at my desk?"

She followed him, and for the next twenty minutes listened to his condolences first, then the raves that he found in her records from all her teachers, but primarily Miss Hawkins. He wanted her to know that from what he had learned about her both as a person, and intellectually, he had a great interest in helping her develop her gift for the written word. Mr. Duncan also reassured her that he was there for her if she ever needed to talk about the tragedy at prom last spring. After giving him obligatory, yet seemingly sincere thanks, Mavis smiled, shook his hand, and made her way back to her desk. It was going to be a long day, and she wouldn't be surprised if it took a week or more for all the sad looks and pitiful questions to become a thing of the past.

Her second-period course was Health and Nutrition, which was temporarily being taught by a sub by the name of Mrs. Meyer. The first thing the woman did was apologize to the survivors of last year's tragedies, told them to focus on the here and now, and then told them they would be moving on in her class as of that very second. Mavis couldn't have been more relieved at how she handled it.

Third-period study hall with Matt consisted mostly of comparing notes from their first two classes regarding staff and students reactions, and then they discussed Matt's plans for providing her with the nourishment her zombie body needed to maintain its non-violent state. He would be working from four each afternoon until eleven at night, at which time he would drop a cooler of fresh meat outside her window that should take care of her the entire following day. It was a good plan, and she felt loved and secure.

Statistics class was like the first of the day, with much grieving and discussion over the prom night massacre and the losses suffered. Her next two classes consisted of Psychology and Early Child Development, taught by Randall and Hayes respectively. Both of these instructors handled things much the same way the sub in Health did, but with much more compassion and patience, and they made themselves available to the students for guidance before beginning first-day break-in introductions.

Finally, in the last period, her second study hall had arrived. Now she would be with both Matt and Kim, and she was anxious to compare the entire day's notes with them. Mavis was even more eager to hear Kim complain about taking Trigonometry again, and she swore to herself that she was going to be harder on Kim about helping her with the work. She would tutor her but no more fixing her messes. If she was going to graduate, it wasn't going to be riding out Trig on Mavis' back.

That last period was very loose for those in study hall, filled with low talking and a bit of light laughter; after all, there was nothing to study yet. Tomorrow would be different, for sure, so Mavis and her friends took advantage of the lazy period, waiting for the bell to ring only in the back of their minds.

But after class, while Kim went to meet Shawn Maher at his truck, and while Mavis and Matt made their way to her car, the strangest thing happened.

They were walking side by side. Matt was telling her an amusing story about some kid in his Journalism class who actually signed up for the elective because he thought he would write in a "diary" all day. It had been a riot, and Matt did a great job telling it. But as they walked and he rambled on, Mavis lost focus and stopped. Something was in the air, and it didn't smell... right.

Matt continued to walk, babbling continuously while Mavis stood, frozen in her spot, sniffing the air around her. What was that? It was so familiar to her, so known... yet there was something off about the scent, something different. The problem was, while the scent was familiar, the "offness" of it was making it terribly hard for her to identify.

"Mavis, are you okay?"

Matt was making his way back to her, concern all over his face. Mavis barely heard his words and didn't acknowledge them at all. She simply kept inhaling over and over, but her mind still couldn't identify whose essence she was picking up on the breeze.

"Mavis! You're freaking me out! What's going on? Is there a fire or something?"

Suddenly, she snapped out of her daze with a jerk of her body, thanks to the firmness and concern in his voice. "What? Wh-What's wrong?"

"What's wrong with you?" Matt asked.

Mavis gave a sigh and a chuckle, then shrugged. "I don't know. I thought I smelled someone I knew... once. I... I just can't remember who it reminded me of because it was… different somehow. No biggie." She grabbed him by the hand and pushed the unsettling occurrence out of her mind. "Let's go; I am so over today!"

Matt picked up where he left off as they walked to the car, and Mavis laughed and acknowledged him in all the right places, but all the while her eyes were moving around the lot trying to pinpoint the human smell that was lingering all around her.

As Matt opened the passenger door for her to get in, the smell faded, and as he got into the driver's seat, Mavis was finally able to push the odor out of her mind and pay all her attention to him.

But at the far end of the lot sat a silver luxury sports car, and the driver was paying close attention to them both. She had her window half-down, and she daydreamed about how she was going to be the downfall of Mavis Harvey.

After all, Mavis not only ruined her life in Greenville, she had turned her into the flesh-eating monster she was today. Revenge would belong to Shanice Hall, no matter what. It was just going to take a bit of time to work out the details of her perfect plan.

But now her stomach was growling. Soon, it would be time for her to feed, and she already had her next meal stalked out.

CHAPTER 6

Shanice Hall looked up from the bloody bones, uninterested in the shreds of flesh and muscle which still hung off them. She wiped her mouth and the back of her sleeve and stood up from where she was kneeling over the dead car salesman's corpse. The sound of rushing blood still filled her ears, and even in the dark shadows of the alley, she could see with sharp clarity. She just loved how she felt when she was eating.

He had been another easy one; it seemed most of them were because they never saw it coming. Here she was, this beautiful young woman, showing up out of nowhere, and sweet talking them all the way to their deaths. That was why she loved dining on the male of the species; it gave her a sense of power that she didn't get when she had female victims. Not to mention the fact that, to her, men just tasted better.

Shanice cast one final look of disdain down at poor Mark Williams, a former car salesman for Supreme Foreign Motors. She glanced over at the rear exit of the business, the door he had come out of when she approached him complaining of an issue with her new luxury sports car overheating. He had been directly under the only light in the alleyway when she approached, and she smiled as she recalled noticing him trying to slyly slip off his wedding band. He was a piece of crap, and he deserved to die.

Making her way towards the alley's dead end where her car was parked, she looked down at her hands; they were tacky with blood, and so were her clothes. She refused to get blood all over the inside of her new baby, so she paused at a puddle and cleaned her hands off as best as she could with the murky water. She stripped off her jacket, then removed her jeans, shoes, and socks. Those items all went into the trunk, wrapped in the jacket, now inside out. Shanice didn't want to mess the trunk's carpeting, either.

As she drove back to her new place to shower and sleep, she thought about Candy. She often thought about Candy since she arrived back in Ohio; the two had been best friends for years. In her own twisted way, Shanice had a strange kind of love and affection for her old friend. But all of that had changed one day in the mouth of an alley, thanks to Mavis Harvey. Not only had that incident been the catalyst for the separation of the two friends, but it had also been the day that Shanice changed into what she was now: a flesh-eating, enraged murderer consumed by such evil that she reveled in her new life role, even if she didn't understand it at all.

Candy Wilkes. She had been intending to get in touch with the girl for a while but hadn't done it yet. Tomorrow she would; she would call Candy at her parents' home, and the two of them would catch up, then she would convince her to join in the fun and games of getting back at Mavis. The only thing Shanice wasn't going to talk to Candy about was the fact that she was going to give her a big bite. The exact same kind of rabid bite that Mavis gave her in that alley the year before. It would be the kind of bite that would turn her into the same monster that Shanice herself had become.

Ten minutes later, Shanice parked in the underground garage beneath her loft's building. She bolted from her car to the lift, clothes in hand and rear end covered only in panties. Soon, she was letting herself into her place; all she could think about was showering and sleeping because she had big plans for the morning.

In the morning, she would take the first step in exacting her revenge on that vixen, Mavis Harvey.

∞

The following week was one of the most tense and crazy of Mavis's life.

The school was her main focus, but she had a terrible time dedicating her attention to it as she should. Thankfully, it had always been fairly easy for her to pull top grades, and she was especially grateful for this during this time. Her mind was constantly on the safety of her family and friends, so she was always on edge, watching and wondering. When it came time to study or learn, she had to force it, so her ability to retain information was especially helpful.

Matt was her biggest supporter, which she knew was a huge load for him as well. Not only did he have school, but he worked part-time in the evenings at the packing house to keep bringing her food. Mavis didn't know what she would do without him.

CHAPTER 7

"Alright! Matt, Todd! Let these ladies get the food set out and ready! Time for us to go a quick round on the mini course!"

Detective Ben Gordon shouted out to the male companions that were in his group of picnickers. The Harveys, his own wife, and his two kids, David, and Cara Gordon were all in the group, and they were making a day of it at Donnelly Park. The two families had socialized ever since Candy Wilkes had gone through the legal system, was sentenced and committed, and was subsequently transferred to the Greenville Psychiatric Hospital. Todd and Ben had become fast friends, as had their wives. While Ben's kids were younger than Mavis, they got along great with the young lady. Ben had grown very close to her as well. Yes, she was off, but it was in a unique way that seemed to fit her "Goth" personality and appearance. Otherwise, Mavis was sensitive, funny, and had a heart that wanted to do and be right at any cost. Ben sensed that she had some sort of chip on her shoulder, but he never pressed her to talk to him about it. He simply let her know he was there for her all the time, whenever she needed him. He felt like an uncle to the girl.

"We're coming!" Todd turned briefly to his wife, who stood smiling and rolling her eyes at Kelly Gordon, who returned the look. "Do you ladies have this? Set up and unloading the food and all, I mean?"

Jane nodded. "Take Matt and David and get out of here, will you?"

Todd started off toward Ben, with Matt and David Gordon right behind him. Cara, Ben's daughter, was already at the cars with Mavis, each of them grabbing something to haul up the grassy hill toward their chosen picnic benches. There was a lot of food to be unloaded, and just as much set up; these outings had proven themselves to last all day.

"I suppose we'd better get busy, Jane," Kelly Gordon said with a sigh. "Even though they are doing the short Frisbee golf course, they'll expect to eat when they get back."

"Yep," Jane replied as she gave a pat to Kelly's shoulder. "Let's do this thing."

For the next forty-five minutes, Mavis, Jane, and Kelly and Cara Gordon got things situated. They were grilling in the park that particular day: steaks for the adults, burgers, and brats for the younger set. There were also both potato and noodle salads, baked beans, cold chicken, a variety of chips, and two large coolers completely filled with cold beverages. Of course, one was for the grown-ups in that situation as well.

During that time, the women started the meat while Mavis and Cara set up the rest of the picnic. Music played from portable Bluetooth speakers, light conversation and laughter were dominant. Time passed freely in the sunlight, and before anyone knew it, Ben, Todd, and the boys were back.

Without being announced at all, everyone began to line up to the table holding plates. They all took turns loading up while everyone laughed and talked in unison, and it wasn't long before all of them were seated and digging in. Various conversations took place between them all, with Mavis trying to include Cara Gordon as best as she could; she hated the thought that the twelve-year-old girl might feel left out in any way.

But then, the strangest thing happened: while Cara filled Mavis in on all the details of her incredibly "hot" biology teacher, Mavis happened to glance toward the woodline. It was only a glance, and not focused on any particular space or area, but her eyes fell directly onto something disturbing. A person wearing a big, floppy hat and sunglasses was seated just behind a bush that served as part of the forest's border. She focused her eyes on the person, but as soon as they realized they had been seen, they disappeared from sight entirely. All she could think about was the incident with Candy Wilkes the summer before, the same incident that resulted in Matt getting shot with a pellet gun and the rear light being shot on her car. Ben was sitting on her right, chatting with Todd about nonsense, so she nudged him in the arm and leaned toward him.

"Ben, someone is watching us in the woods," she whispered.

He turned to her with a slight look of alarm on his face. "Where?"

"Straight ahead," she replied with a nod in the direction.

Without another word, Ben rose and made his way to the woodline. As he approached, he immediately noticed the ruffling of the leaves as the culprit scrambled on their hands and knees to get away from the scene. Ben could just barely make out the rounded top of some kind of hat, which motivated him to step into the woods to make the chase. But before he knew it, the spy had disappeared completely from sight.

He made his way back to the group, all of whom had ceased to enjoy their meal and had their eyes focused on him to wait for the verdict.

"Well, it was nothing," Ben said lightly with a smile as he took his seat once again. "Probably just some kid who wanted to spook us out a bit."

He gave Mavis a glance and a smile, which she returned, but she wasn't convinced. Hat and glasses, or not, this person rang the bell of familiarity in her head. She continued to eat and tried to push the incident out of her mind as much as she could, but even as she resumed the laughter and conversations taking place around her, the sight of the spy continued to tug at the back of her mind.

Mavis had a very uneasy feeling that whoever it had been, they were watching her and the others intently, and with a strong sense of purpose.

Shanice Hall tossed the ugly hat onto the passenger seat of her luxury sports car as she sped out of Donnelly Park. She had definitely been spotted by Little Miss Do-Good, but she was convinced that Mavis had in no way been able to pinpoint her identity. She began to laugh out loud as she ran her hand through her long, dark hair while she steered the car with the other.

Well, well, well. It looked as though her archenemy had been enjoying life to the fullest. When Shanice thought about the fact that Mavis had been able to turn her into a monster with just one bite, she had no doubt that the girl had also made a meal out of Jeff Deason. Although she didn't go to the Junior Winter Formal due to relocation, she'd heard about the similar death of Colin Handley, who happened to be one of Shanice's favorite crushes. The way it sounded through the family grapevine, she was also sure that Mavis had dined on him as well. The fury toward her nemesis was building up inside her as she pulled the coupe into the garage.

But as she rode the lift up to her loft and considered that fury, along with the bigger picture, the one she had in mind of her desired end result of the situation, she began to calm herself. No, she wouldn't lose it on Mavis herself... she would do it ingeniously and systematically.

She would begin by taking out the ones Mavis loved the most.

It was now a full week since she had eaten the salesman. Her intent for the morning after the incident had been to track down Candy and have a little talk with her old friend. They would plot and scheme Mavis' demise, and together they would carry it out until the end. But none of this would take place before Shanice gifted Candy with the change.

Up to this point, her search had been fruitless. When she first contacted Mr. and Mrs. Wilkes, they were less than forthcoming regarding Candy's whereabouts. She wasn't living at home, and she wasn't speaking to anyone from her hometown. Shanice asked for an address to which she could write, but they said her location was to be kept confidential for her own well-being. Shanice knew that it didn't help the situation for them to know it was her; they hated her immensely, even though they maintained a pleasant, if not curt, façade. Unfortunately, she had told them who she was as soon as Mrs. Wilkes answered the telephone. The entire conversation went south from there.

During personal consideration, after showering and preparing for bed, Shanice had dined on leftovers from a 26-year-old construction worker she killed recently. Shanice thought about her next step and what it should be. Was Candy being kept in a group home? Was she possibly in some kind of juvenile prison? Perhaps the Wilkeses had actually seen fit to adopt her to another family. Shanice had no clue; the fact of the matter was that, while she had always been the leader, Candy had always been the coldest, in her own crazy way. Maybe she just went off the deep end, and her family sent her to some kind of boot camp or something.

Tucking herself into bed, Shanice yawned and

settled in. In the morning, she would get on her laptop and do a bit of searching for her old pal. If she was out there, and she was still Candy Wilkes of Greenville, then Shanice would find her. Smiling to herself with arrogant confidence, Shanice drifted off into a restless sleep.

CHAPTER 8

While Shanice Hall snored lightly in her fitful slumber, Mavis lay in her own bed, the soft light of her bedside lamp casting a halo to her right. The television was tuned to a movie she had seen several times, and she paid no attention to it. Mavis had two things on her mind, and the first was a mild one: Matt would be at the back window soon with her breakfast for the morning, and she looked forward to seeing him.

But the second wasn't so comforting. Mavis was mostly thinking about the girl in the woods at Donnelly Park. There was something about her that was familiar, but she couldn't quite put her finger on it. It was just out of her reach.

Donnelly Park was where Candy had hidden in the woods, in much the same way, and shot Matt during summer break. Just the sight of someone lurking disturbed Mavis to no end, but what made it worse was the fact that she was positive she knew the person: the disguise made it impossible to be certain.

Suddenly, Mavis' cell rang, and she nearly jumped out of her skin.

"Hello?"

She heard a chuckle. "Hey, babe. It's Matt. Were you sleeping? Did I scare you awake?"

"I was awake, just waiting for you," she replied. "But you still scared me. What's up? I thought you'd be here by now."

"That's why I'm calling," he said, a bit of regret in his voice. "I have to actually work until two in the morning to fill in for some guy whose wife is having a baby. Sorry. But listen, I'll drop the cooler off outside your window on my way home. Just get some rest."

She was almost flooded with relief; Mavis was exhausted. "Oh! No, Matt, that's fine. I'm really pretty beat anyway. I hope you have a good night."

"I love you, Mav," he said in a husky voice.

Mavis smiled. "I love you, too, Big Guy."

The pair disconnected the call and then began to settle in. Plugging her phone into her charger, she then fluffed her pillow, settled into its soft support, and turned off the television and bedside light.

As she began to drift off, thinking of Matt and his soft words, the phone rang again, this time seeming atrociously loud in the black silence of the room. Mavis shot straight up and grabbed it; in her daze, she tried to answer it quickly just to shut it up.

"Hello?" Even her voice was groggy.

There was a moment of silence, then, "Oh, did I wake you, Mavis? I'd hate to think I did."

Who was this? Kim? Mavis shook her head to clear it and tried again.

"Kim, is this you?"

A brief girlish giggle was all Mavis got in return at first. Then: "Don't you remember my voice? Well, let's face it, it has been a while. I must say, you sound exactly the same as I remember."

Mavis was wide awake now, her mind racing. She narrowed her eyes in thought, thankful that the room was so dark, blocking out distractions.

"Candy, is this you?"

Now the girl on the other end laughed out loud, almost guffawing. Mavis hated games; she found them to be a pointless waste of time. "No. Now, you know Candy wouldn't be able to give you a call; she doesn't even live at home anymore. No one seems to know where Candy is. I was sleeping soundly, then I woke and realized, hey, she might not be spot on, but I bet Mavis knows where Candy is."

Mavis froze… it was Shanice, and she didn't sound like the Shanice Mavis had once gone to school with. She sounded… more evil than ever.

"Why would I know?"

Shanice paused. "Because you do, so knock off the crap. I want to know where she is, Mavis."

Without even so much as a pause, Mavis whispered in a voice filled with contempt, "You're Shanice. What do you want? Where have you come from?"

The girl on the other end of the phone cackled with delight. "Where have I come from? Well, you should know. I come from that far-away place that you had me driven to… that place that took me away from Greenville. What a stupid question, 'Where did you come from?' It seems to me that we have much to catch up on, but now is not the time. Where is Candy?"

Mavis didn't hesitate but quickly swiped the screen of her cell phone and hung up on the call. Shanice! So, she hadn't disappeared off the face of the Earth after all! Had it been her at the park today? Where had she come back from, and why was she so intent on finding Candy? It seemed to Mavis that Candy had much bigger problems to deal with on her plate than the ones Shanice's presence would inevitably bring.

Her phone rang again, and this time she answered it part-way through the first ring.

"I'm going to tell you something, Mavis," Shanice sneered as soon as she answered. "I'm going to find Candy, and I'm going to see to it that you pay for what you have done to me. You mark my words."

Mavis was starting to get pissed. "I did nothing to you; every consequence you suffered you brought onto yourself."

Another laugh, but this time it was filled with evil anger. "Oh, you really have no idea. But don't worry; the worst of it has turned out to be the very best for me. You'll see, Mavis… you'll see."

This time Shanice hung up on her, and the phone went dead in her hand. She turned off the ringer and sat staring at the clock on her nightstand: it was past midnight. Mavis couldn't believe that after all this time Shanice Hall had returned, and she seemed bent on making Mavis pay for her problems. Should she call Detective Gordon and tell him of the calls? No, not until morning. It was Monday tomorrow, and she would be able to talk to him in detail, but it was just too late now to wake him and his family.

Slowly, Mavis got back under her blankets, but no matter how hard she tried, she couldn't get comfortable. For the rest of the night, she tossed and turned, her mind racing over the calls. But she was also powerless to do anything but lie and fret, and it wasn't until nearly four in the morning that she finally fell asleep, even missing Matt putting her cooler outside the bedroom window.

She dreamed of Shanice, coming for her and trying to eat her, and all she could do was fight and fight… and fight.

∞

Just as she had planned, Shanice spent most of the following morning researching Candy Wilkes and her possible whereabouts.

As she typed and read, read and typed, she thought about the call she had put in to Mavis in the middle of the night, and Shanice began to laugh all over again. What a weak little bug! Did she have no idea of the depth of misery she had caused Shanice? From what she discovered on the Internet, Mavis had done the same to Candy. Oh, she would have her revenge, and so would her presumed-insane best friend. Oh, Candy would have it in spades.

From what Shanice could find, Candy had been blamed for the murders of not only Jeff Deason, but of Colin and most of the junior class at prom last year.

Articles mentioned that Shanice was assumed to have been involved, but had managed to fall off the radar. Now, Candy was locked up at Greenville Psych for an undetermined amount of time, and Shanice was furious.

As for her, yes, she had disappeared. When her father caught her eating a neighborhood cat, and then when she tried to bite the head maid on the neck, he was at the end of his rope. They moved to Tuscany, changed their last name, and Shanice began to see a psychiatrist for her strange behavior. He wasn't that great of a shrink, but Shanice would readily admit that the man had tasted extraordinary.

Now, here she was in America, her parents both dead because of the appetites Mavis had bestowed upon her, and she was ready to take care of the mess that her enemy had made, and a big mess it was. The only thing she had to figure out now was how to get to Candy and have some time alone with her. The Wilkeses would never grant special permission for her to visit her friend; she was going to have to pose as an aunt or another type of family member or clergy. It wouldn't take much to figure out what to do, but she would have to do some serious thinking in order to come up with the right plan.

Shanice's stomach gave a slight growl. It wasn't too bad; usually, she had always eaten her daily meals at night, which enabled her to get through the following day. She wondered how Mavis did it, Mavis the flesh-eater who thought it wise to share her gift. It didn't matter; Shanice had herself to worry about. Anyway, she always kept some leftovers to tide her over through the day, if needed. It seemed it was needed now, and she was thankful for the heart and kidneys she had stashed in the fridge. When she was done eating, she would make a call to Greenville Psych and get some visiting information.

As she chewed on the heart, and very slowly, she thought about how she was going to bite Candy, how she was going to change her. Shanice knew she couldn't do it right there in the institution in front of other people. She would have to do it from the outside, which meant that she would have to get her friend out of there somehow. That should be simple enough, though. She would take a wig, a change of clothing, and some extra makeup. If they had even fifteen minutes alone, she would help Candy get changed, and they would stroll out of there together like nothing.

Shanice pulled the bloody organ to her mouth and tore right in, as all thoughts of Candy Wilkes escaped out of her mind.

CHAPTER 9

First thing Monday morning, Mavis put in a call to Detective Gordon. She spoke with Matt when he showed up early to have breakfast with her and her mother and filled him in on all the details of Shanice's calls from the previous night. It didn't take him long to get upset, and he insisted she makes the call to Ben. They ended up making an appointment for Ben to meet the kids in the parking lot at Westside during their lunch period to discuss the details.

As for Matt, he didn't know Shanice (or Candy, for that matter), having been the new kid during the second semester. By the time he was enrolled and attending, the two of them were no more than rumors of the past, and exaggerated ones, at that. What he did know is that a single incident between Mavis and the girls, in an alley, just less than a full year ago, had managed to affect a lot of families and people's lives. As far as he was concerned, Matt didn't have a kind thought toward her, even though she was a stranger to him.

So, like robots, the two of them went through their day, quiet and introspective, speaking really to no one other than each other. By the time lunch period arrived, they couldn't get to the parking lot to wait for Ben fast enough. Fortunately, they didn't have to wait at all; he was parked directly at the bottom of the steep concrete staircase that led to the main entrance doors.

"Hop in, kids," Ben greeted them. "I'll buy you lunch."

Matt climbed into the front, while Mavis got comfortable in the seat right behind him. Ben didn't pull any punches whatsoever; they were still in the parking lot buckling their safety belts when he dove right in. Neither Mavis nor Matt was surprised.

"So, let's talk about what happened, Mavis," the detective and friend said bluntly.

She took a deep breath. "I was settling in for bed. My phone rang and jostled me awake. I answered, and a female voice started to ask me weird questions. She wanted to know about Candy Wilkes and where she was… what happened to her. She was spooky and rude, and downright condescending."

Ben drove in the direction of the closest Sports Burger. "Did she tell you she was Shanice?"

"No," Mavis replied simply. "I asked her."

Ben pulled the sedan up into the drive-thru line right behind a beat-up car. "So, she admitted it? I mean, directly?"

"Well," Mavis muttered as she recalled the conversation. "It was more like I told her, 'This is Shanice', and she basically continued in the conversation taking on that role… I mean, she didn't deny it."

Ben pulled up as the car in front and started giving

their order to the lady running the speaker system. "You didn't tell her where Candy was, I take it?"

"No, Ben. There is no way I would have even considered it."

Gordon nodded. "Now do your dad and mom know about this?"

Mavis and Matt exchanged glances, and then she looked at Ben and shook her head.

"Okay, so I guess from here you're both going to go home; I'll call the school myself. We will talk to your parents together. Matter of fact, I'll join you for a bit."

Mavis groaned. Her mother was going to have a coronary! Just when her family and friends were beginning to relax after all of the chaos of the Candy Wilkes ordeal over the summer, now this happened. It was even worse because this was Shanice they were talking about! Candy was nothing compared to her! Jane would likely put her immediately under lock and key.

After they ordered their food and pulled up a notch in line, Ben took advantage of the wait time to call Westside, identify himself, and let the administrative faculty know that both Mavis Harvey and Matt Morgan would not be attending the remainder of the day's classes. Both kids sat in silence as he took care of the task.

Fifteen minutes later, the three of them were seated at the Harvey dining room table, eating sandwiches and fries. Ben had ordered two chicken sandwiches, one he obviously intended to share with Jane, should she want it. While the foursome ate, the conversation began, with

Ben's prompting, of course.

"So, Mavis, I think you have something you need to share with your mother," he began. "I'm here for support, as I'm sure Matt is if you need us."

Jane immediately almost choked on a bit of her Chicken Supreme sandwich. Once she safely swallowed her half-eaten bite, she turned to her daughter with a stern look on her face. "Now what, Mavis? We've had such peace around here. Did Candy Wilkes escape from the nut house or something?"

This time when Mavis groaned, she did it aloud. "No, Mother. It really has nothing to do with Candy… at least, not that much so far, anyway."

Jane put down her sandwich and rested her elbows on the table. Leaning forward and giving Ben Gordon a piercing stare, she asked, "What is she talking about, Ben?"

If the detective had thought he would be escaping the limelight of this conversation, he had been dead wrong. "Well, Jane, it seems that Mavis got a call late last night from someone who we suspect was Shanice Hall, and we have reason to believe she could be in town."

Now a look of confusion came over the woman's face. "At this point in time, what does that even mean to any of us? And why would she be here?"

Ben opened his mouth to reply, but Mavis cut him off. "She wanted to know where Candy was, and she was less than friendly about it, Mom. As a matter of fact, she was pretty sinister. Something about her was…

off."

Now it was Ben's turn to look confused. "You didn't mention this in the car. What do you mean, 'off?'"

Mavis shrugged. "Well, she has always been mean and spiteful, sort of hateful in all her ways. But on the phone last night she sounded like... like she had changed for the worse. I can't put a finger on her, but it's like she went away bad and came back a demon or something."

The table was quiet for several minutes. Matt slowly nibbled at a fry, while both Mavis and Jane stared down at their food. Ben Gordon's was long gone, having eaten when he wasn't talking. Finally, Jane spoke in a low, steady voice filled with concern.

"Does the reappearance of Shanice pose some kind of threat?" She directed the question at Ben directly.

He gave her an earnest look. "We can't know that yet, Jane. The truth is I'm going to be up half the night trying to figure out where the Halls are living now just so I can get in touch with the parents and try to piece things together. I would suggest that the kids stay indoors and out of sight until I am able to gather some more information."

At that very moment, Todd walked into the kitchen. His hand was at his tie, loosening it. His hair was tousled, and he looked like he could fall asleep standing up. Everyone at the table looked up at him, and he looked at them.

"What's going on?"

Ben chuckled. "Have a seat, Todd. I'll run to Sports Burger and grab you a Grand Slam Meal; Jane and the kids can fill you in."

Ben was back with Todd's food in twenty short minutes, and never had he received such an energetic welcome from his new friend. For one thing, Todd was starving, and for another, he was completely beside himself with the information about Shanice.

Unfortunately, he was told the same thing as the others: until Shanice either made any of her motives clear, or Ben had a chance to track down and talk to the Hall family, it was hard to know what was going on. So, for the next several hours, Ben remained with the family discussing the situation, giving advice, and making phone calls to his office so his secretary could issue an all-points on Shanice Hall. The time passed quickly, and it wasn't until nearly eight that evening that Ben was even able to consider heading home to his family.

∞

Two hours earlier, Shanice was pulling into the parking lot at Greenville Psychiatric. It was nothing like she expected, considering that Candy was being held for murder. The place had minimal security; there wasn't even a guard at the parking entrance. It looked just like any other business or medical facility: no fences, no guards, and no bars on the windows or doors. In Shanice's mind, that meant there were only a couple of ways they were keeping Candy there. They were either doping her up but good, or Candy was staying due to the threat of true imprisonment. Either way, she was sure that this was going to be much easier than she had initially thought.

Parking her car as near to the main entrance as possible, she grabbed her large hobo bag carrying the wig, clothes, and makeup and made her way to the door. When she opened it and stepped inside, she was met with all the smells and sounds one would expect inside such a place. Cries and sobs rang through the halls, people shuffled around, and the aroma of excrement mingled with those of the varieties of flesh that Shanice had come to detect so easily in the last year.

"Can I help you, ma'am?"

Shanice turned to her left to see a nurse standing behind a large, tall desk area. The woman was smiling, and even though Shanice could detect the smells of lavender and vanilla wafting from her flesh, she also had the slight aroma of bacon. Fighting her urges, she smiled back at the nurse and approached her.

"Yes, I'm here to visit my niece."

The woman maintained her smile and reached for a clipboard. "That's fine; we love having visitors for the patients. It speeds their recovery along wonderfully. Who are you here to see?"

"Candy Wilkes, please."

Now the nurse's smile faltered, but only slightly. "I'm pleased. Miss Wilkes really hasn't had any visitors since her parents stopped coming. You are her aunt?"

Shanice nodded. "Yes... her father's sister."

"I'll have to ask what you have in the bag, ma'am," the nurse said with a glance at the object. "No weapons, drugs, or contraband of any kind is permitted during visitation."

"Oh, I fully understand, especially considering the reason she is here." Shanice removed the bag from her shoulder. "It's just my purse, actually. Would you like to search for it?"

The nurse shook her head and smiled once again. "I don't think that will be necessary. I'll just need you to fill out the visitors' roster here." She slid the clipboard toward Shanice. "By the way, I just love your suit."

Shanice had chosen a crisp, finely detailed suit because it made her look completely businesslike and professional. She knew it would throw off any doubters, and that was what she wanted. She really didn't have any time for hold-ups.

"Thank you very much," she replied, beaming with pride. "It's one of my favorites."

She set about filling out the form's required single line, listing her name as Caroline Wilkes-Barringer, aunt of the patient. The address and phone number she gave were completely fabricated, and she didn't even have to think about them as she jotted them down.

When she was finished, she asked, "Is there a visitation room I will be meeting her in?"

"Visitation room?" The nurse chuckled slightly. "Oh, my, no. That would be the case if Candace were an adult, but our juvenile offender patients are able to have family visits in their rooms. Her room number is 247. Just take the elevator there to the second floor, exit to the left, and it will be the last room at the end of the hall."

"Thank you."

"I'll call up now and make sure that the ward nurse has her in her room, waiting."

Shanice gave a single nod with her forced smile and made her way to the elevator. In less than thirty seconds, she was exiting the same and came face to face with a nurses' station manned by a single woman who appeared to be watching a television soap opera. Professionalism at its finest. The woman turned to her, appearing annoyed at the distraction.

"Candy Wilkes, please?"

The woman snorted. "Room 247, at the end of the hall." She turned back to the television. This was going to be much easier than Shanice thought.

She made her way down the hall, and when she reached the room, she stood there, staring at the numbers on it, just under the small square observation window, for several seconds. Look what they had done to her loyal minion. They had locked her up for things she hadn't done, and they were someday planning to put her in prison. Well, it wasn't going to happen.

After a quick glance over her shoulder to see who was paying attention, she grasped the doorknob and opened the door. Stepping inside, Shanice closed it behind her. Candy was sitting in an ugly orange vinyl chair with wood armrests; she was staring dumbly out the window, and it seemed to Shanice that Candy hadn't even heard her come in. She was surely on some kind of dope.

"Candy."

Slowly, her friend turned around and looked at her. Her stare of disbelief seemed to last forever, her mouth open wide as she obviously struggled to believe her own eyes. Shanice just smiled at her.

"Sh-Shanice?"

With a nod, she replied, "It's me, Candy, and I've come to set everything right." She crossed the room and sat on the edge of the bed, placing a hand on Candy's shoulder. "Now, we don't have a lot of time, so listen carefully…"

∞

"Mavis, look!" she glanced in the direction Matt was pointing. There, on the coffee table, was the daily paper. On the front page, in bold black letters, it read "Westside Ravager Escapes from Greenville Psych." The subtitle went on to say that Candy Wilkes was nowhere to be found after a visit from a woman posing as her aunt.

"Oh, Matt…"

∞

"I'm hungry, Shanice." Candy was whining a bit, and the growls coming from her stomach were deafening. "It hurts, I'm so hungry!"

Shanice had already let the girl eat what brain she had saved, and she had even gone so far as to break out some intestines she had hoarded from another one of her victims. But none of it seemed to satisfy Candy, who seemed to have no interest in controlling her growing appetite.

"Look, Candy, I know how you feel, but you have to learn to control it, or you're going to wind up getting us both in major trouble." She sat down next to her friend, who was beginning to look the part more and more every second. Her skin was paling quickly, and the dark circles under her eyes and patches of dry skin were really starting to show. "Besides, we have other things to worry about right now. For one, we have to dye your hair; the color it is right now makes you look like death warmed over. We also have to get some makeup on you, so you don't look so… ill. So, put all of this out of your mind about eating and let's get busy."

She grabbed her friend by the arm and jerked her to her feet. Candy gave a whine and followed Shanice to the bathroom. For the next two hours, they set about making Candy over, so her "condition" wasn't so obvious. Shanice didn't have high hopes; Candy simply wasn't as beautiful as she was, though she did hold her own when she was all cleaned up and dressed up. Well, not everyone could be so perfect.

While Shanice worked the dye through Candy's hair with her fingertips, the girl asked, "So, what you are saying is that we are, like, zombies?"

Shanice stopped in her tracks. "Yeah, I guess so. That's exactly what we are!" Why hadn't she realized it before? She ate people, craved flesh and blood, and constantly thought about killing others for food. She was made this way by a bite delivered to her… it all made sense.

Shanice spun Candy around on the closed toilet to face her. "Yes, Candy, we are zombies. If we get caught doing anything like what we did last night, they are going to bury bullets in our brains, just like in the movies. So, I don't care how hungry you get, you do things my way. We are in this to get back at Mavis, remember? This isn't just about snacking all the damn time." She gave her another rough spin and went back to fingering the dye job. "Just listen to me, and you'll be fine… we'll both be fine."

While she continued to work on her friend, her mind raced with the realization. If she was a zombie, she couldn't die… she would live forever, unless someone took her head off, anyway. That would be a long shot because the fact was that no one would know she was a zombie, so they wouldn't know what to do to stop her. All she had to do was not get caught carrying out her plans.

Shanice wouldn't get caught; she was just too good for that. Mavis was going to pay for all that happened to her and Candy. Yes, Mavis was going to get what was coming to her, all right.

∞

Ben walked to his car from the office, he yawned, long and hard. Oh, he was tired. It amazed him that he had allowed himself to get so relaxed regarding the Wilkes case when there was a loose end like Shanice Hall involved. Sure, he had been continuing on in his investigation of the girl and her whereabouts, but since he had continued to run into brick walls at every turn, he had only given half-effort. It looked like he'd really dropped the ball on that one.

He figured he would do a visual drive by the Harvey house on his way home, just to ease his nerves. With all the murders happening, he was a nervous wreck. He drove two blocks up from the Harveys' and stopped at a stop sign just in time to yawn again. The road was empty except for his vehicle, he noted as he looked to the right. But when he glanced to the left, he saw another vehicle sitting just out from under the dome of light from the streetlight above. The car was in the shadows, but he could still make out two forms, both appearing to be female. One was fishing around in the open trunk while the other was kneeling next to the rear tire; it looked to him like they had a flat.

His cop's instinct didn't allow him to think; he simply acted. Immediately, Ben took the left turn and slowly approached the car. As he neared, he could see that the unfortunate pair consisted of two females, and they looked fairly young, though it was hard to tell due to the fact that they wore baseball caps on their heads, shadowing their features even more than the darkness already did.

The girl at the trunk turned to look in his direction, but the one on the ground barely gave a glance. Ben slowed his car and rolled down the passenger window. The girl at the trunk looked over at him and offered a smile.

"Flat tire?" he asked.

She nodded.

"I don't mind lending a hand if you like."

The girl gave another nod, and Ben backed his car up, parking it along the curb behind them, directly under the street lamp. He jumped out of the car and started toward them. Once again, the girl at the tire hardly moved, while the other turned fully to him. Where had he seen her before?

"Do you have everything you need?" His mind was racing as he tried to place her face. "Jack? Spare? Crowbar?"

"Everything?" she purred. "I just need help getting the spare out if you don't mind. We can do the rest."

Ben walked up to the trunk. "No problem."

As soon as he arrived at the open compartment, the first thing he noticed was the fact that there was no tire inside. He glanced here and there, squinting in the darkness before turning and saying, "Is it beneath the carpet panel?"

Those were the last words Ben Gordon ever spoke. Shanice Hall and the newly-zombified Candy Wilkes were on him faster than flies on spoiled chicken. They bit at him, tearing his flesh and chewing with delight as blood shot from his neck in great spurts. He screamed, but only for a second right in the beginning. It didn't take him long to collapse to the ground after that, and it was only seconds later that he gave his final twitch and died.

The pair finished eating right there in the shadows, and then Shanice proceeded to bag up his liver and part of his brain to take home for the morning. Candy sat and watched her in silence, licking Ben's blood from her fingers as she did. It had to be the best feeling in the world, she thought as Shanice worked.

"So, you think Mavis will know?"

Shanice snorted and slammed the organs safely away into the trunk. "Of course; I know she'll know. It might take a minute to put it together in her pea brain, but it won't take too long."

So, they left, Ben Gordon's stripped corpse lying in a puddle of his own blood just out from under the street lamp light. He wouldn't be found until dawn when a Greenville patrolman pulled down the dead-end to drink coffee and trap morning speeders.

Shanice and Candy, on the other hand, drove to the loft, full, content, and laughing; Phase I of Operation: Mavis had been fulfilled successfully.

CHAPTER 10

Tuesday morning was a sunny, peaceful morning, the kind that made a student happy that they were going to school because the sunlight filled you with energy and motivation. Just like now, Mavis sat in second period Health and Nutrition, reading the first and second chapters of her textbook and answering the recap questions at the end of each. Her mind was on nothing but her work, that is, until the principal, Mr. Pearson, came over the intercom to interrupt her thoughts.

"Excuse me, Mrs. Meyer; I'll need Mavis Harvey to report to the office immediately, please."

Mavis looked up at the speaker near the ceiling as though the man himself were hanging from a hook up there. She then cast a glance at Mrs. Meyer, who gave her a nod to excuse her. Gathering her books quickly, Mavis made her way out of the classroom and rushed toward the administrative offices near the main entrance of the building.

All the while she walked, she considered what this could be about. Nothing good, that was for sure. Had her mother or father, or even Grandma Cabot, had some kind of accident? It couldn't be Matt or Kim; she knew both of them, and Shawn as well was here at school. Was she in some kind of trouble? Was Ben there to talk to her about a new development regarding Shanice and Candy? Worry filled her heart, and she picked up the pace.

Upon entering the secretarial area, all eyes fell upon her. She stopped just inside the door and looked around the room. After fighting against the self-consciousness that seemed to have momentarily taken over, she took three steps and stopped at the head secretary's desk. It was the same one as always, Mrs. Benson. Fortunately for the fifty-something-year-old woman, she had opted out of chaperoning the Junior Prom at the end of last year. She was now considered "one of the survivors" behind her back on a regular basis.

The woman stood from her desk and removed her antique-framed reading glasses from her face, letting them dangle from the silver chain around her neck. "Mr. Pearson needs to see you, Mavis. If you just have a seat, he'll be with you shortly."

For the first time in Mavis' high school career, the woman seemed almost… compassionate. She was definitely not condescending, as per usual. She was almost… sad, at least that was the feeling Mavis got from her that morning.

"Thank you," Mavis replied suspiciously as she allowed a flicker of a smile, which was little more than a facial tick, of sorts. She took a seat on the hardwood, pew-like bench and placed her books beside her gingerly. Once again, Mavis allowed her eyes to scan the room; each time she made eye contact with one of the office workers, they looked away in haste. Something was definitely wrong.

In only seconds, which seemed like minutes, Mr. Pearson's office door opened, and he glanced out at Mavis, avoiding eye contact at all costs. "Miss Harvey... thank you for your expeditious arrival. Please, come inside."

He stood back and held the door open for her as she grabbed her books and made her way into his office.

"Make yourself comfortable, Miss Harvey." Mr. Pearson moved nervously around his desk and sat down. "Um, we really haven't had the chance to talk, Miss Harvey. I apologize for that."

Mavis almost immediately felt the pressure fall from her shoulders. "Oh! I thought I was in some kind of trouble, Mr. Pearson! Or that something terrible had happened! Wow, what a relief, Sir. I can't even tell you!"

The man picked up a pen that was made to look like a golf club. Mavis noticed that a holder shaped like a golf bag was near her on the edge of the desk. In it remained a pen with a gold golf ball on end, a gold tee on another, and one with a flag. Obviously, the club pen, which he was genuinely fidgeting with right then, went with the rest of the set.

"Um, Miss Harvey, it's not quite so simple. This isn't a social meeting, though at this point I certainly wish it was." Mr. Pearson stopped and cleared his throat. "You see, there has been something of an... emergency situation. Your father is on his way to meet with you, here in my office, of course."

Mavis didn't even realize how much her body immediately stiffened at his words, and she didn't have time to think about it. A sudden knock at the principal's office door jolted her, and she spun in the direction of the sound with wide eyes and sweat on her cold brow.

"Enter, please," Mr. Pearson's controlled voice said.

Todd Harvey came into the room, nodded at the principal, and then thanked the man for his kindness and leniency on this occasion. He then took a seat next to Mavis and continued to direct his eyes on Mr. Pearson.

"Sir, have you said anything about the current circumstances to my daughter as of yet?"

Mr. Pearson shook his head but once. "No, sir. I simply brought her up to meet with you."

"Thank you," Todd replied. He paused and looked at Mavis with a loving smile. "Do you think it's possible that Mavis and I could have a few moments alone?"

"Absolutely, Sir," the principal replied, jumping from his desk and heading for the door. "Take as long as you need… please."

After the office door closed, Mavis immediately spoke, without any sort of hesitation.

"Who is it, Dad?"

Todd took his daughter by her hand. "Mavis, this morning a Greenville patrol officer found a body on the dead-end at Hoyden Street."

"Hoyden Street? By our house?"

Todd nodded. "Just a couple of blocks down, by the first stop sign." He paused. "They found a body there. It had been... ravaged, like Colin, Mavis. It... it... it was Ben Gordon."

"What do you mean? Uncle Ben?" Mavis screamed hysterically. "No!"

Todd nodded and continued to hold her hand.

Mavis simply looked at him as her eyes burned for tears that would likely never come. She couldn't wrap her mind around it at first: ravaged? Like Colin had been?

She threw herself into her father's arms and sobbed tearless sobs that at least allowed her to grieve. Her father held her tight and smoothed down her long black hair and told her it was going to be alright, that he understood how she felt.

But he was relating to the humanity of the situation; he was relating to the fact that she and Ben had formed a bond, just as he had with Ben. He wasn't in any way considering the fact that Mavis knew much more about what was going on than he did... much more than he could imagine.

After ten minutes, Mavis sat back and wiped her eyes with her jacket sleeve for effect. She squared her eyes at Todd and said, "Take me home, Daddy. Please."

Together, they left the principal's office and made their way to the Harvey home. There, Mavis would contact Matt, and tell him to come straight over after school, she would fill him in on what had happened, and together, they could try to figure out what to do next.

CHAPTER 11

Jane and Todd, along with Mavis, ended up spending much of the remainder of the day at the Gordon house. Kelly Gordon and the kids were beside themselves with grief; the kids hid in their rooms mostly, but their tears and sobs could be heard clearly throughout the house. Kelly, would break down for several moments, then pull herself together long enough to make several phone calls before breaking down again. Family and friends, including officers from the police station, trickled in and out of the home in a steady stream, offering assistance in any way they were needed.

The worst part was when Kelly had to go identify Ben at the morgue. Jane and Mavis went with her, but Mavis didn't actually go in for the identification process. Her mother later told her that it was horrible and that Ben Gordon was completely unrecognizable. The only reason Kelly was able to get the task done was because of his wedding band and a necklace that he never took off, which dangled around his exposed spine like something from a horror movie. Mavis couldn't imagine it, and she found herself hating what she was more than ever. This was the kind of pain she had caused most all of Greenville last year, and it made her sick to her stomach.

Todd and Jane decided to stay with Kelly until her mother got in from Indiana to be with her and the kids. Todd would pick up Kelly's mother from the airport, and Jane would cook and help around the house until then. So, on the way back to the house from the morgue, Mavis was dropped off at home to wait for Matt to get out of school. She had already texted him and told him there was an emergency and to please come right over with her car. True to form, less than ten minutes after classes would have been dismissed, Matt was at the door.

"Mav, what's going on?" he asked as soon as she opened the front door.

She didn't answer, she only threw herself into his arms and began to sob tearlessly. Matt held her and comforted her right there on the doorstep until she calmed down enough for them to go inside. He got her sat down on the sofa, brought her some water, then sat next to her.

"Now, what is happening?"

Mavis could only look at him with sadness. "It's Ben. He's been killed, Matt. Not just killed, but eaten."

"It has to be a zombie, but it wasn't me, so who could it be, Shanice? Could she be a zombie, like me?" Mavis winced.

The two of them sat in silence as their minds tried to sort things out.

As she pondered her suspicions, Matt spoke.

"Mavis, look."

He thought for a brief moment. "We're going to take things a step at a time, the first step consisting of finding out where she is living. Ben was in the process of trying to find her family, just like he was saying last night. The obvious course is to begin by doing the same. I'm going to get your laptop."

As Matt went back to Mavis' room, she sat in stunned silence. If this was all true, and if Shanice was there for the sole purpose of causing her and her loved-ones harm, all of them were in danger. It was up to her to protect them because she was the only one Shanice wouldn't be able to hurt.

But she had absolutely no idea where to begin…

∞

Candy Wilkes' escape from the mental institution seemed to be the talk of Greenville. People were nearly in hysterics, convinced that the girl was going to go on a murderous rampage of some kind. The parks were empty of children, and even the adults seemed to be looking over their shoulders with every step they took.

But Mavis and her boyfriend weren't afraid. With each passing minute, they found themselves more and more eager to find out where Shanice was, where Candy was, and where both of them had holed up.

There was also another killing that came out in the news. A car salesman at a foreign motors company had been killed in the alley behind the business, but like Ben Gordon, he hadn't simply been murdered. He had been eaten, with the flesh stripped from his bones and some of his internal organs completely gone. Now police themselves were in a panic; they knew the killer was human because forensics positively identified human tooth marks on his bones. The small suburb of Greenville was on the lookout for a cannibal. There was even talk that the murders which took place the previous year consisted of the same characteristics, and now they were going to be exhuming some of the bodies to look for further evidence. The entire place was in an uproar.

∞

The next six days were filled with chaos, tension, and dread. Fear had gripped the entire city of Toledo and the suburb of Greenville.

The killings continued, and not one time were the bodies hidden. They were left out in the open to be found almost immediately each time. Once there was even a telephone call put into police which directed them to the victims. Shanice and her sidekick wanted the cops to find the bodies, and they wanted to instill fear into the hearts of the citizens of the area. A curfew was set for everyone, adults and youngsters alike, and the buddy system was encouraged on a level that could be considered demanding. Demand wasn't needed, though; most everyone was taking care of their day-to-day business and then going home and locking themselves inside, doing nothing more than peeking out the windows until the following day.

On Sunday morning, another pair of high school

students were found. They weren't together (the boy was discovered beneath a tree on a side street in Greenville; the girl in her own front yard in Toledo), signifying that the murders were either committed separately, or they were done together, and then the bodies were tossed out like trash. There was no sign that the pair had any connection or knew each other in any way.

On Monday, a brother and sister were discovered on the community college campus. Their parents had called the police around midnight on Sunday to report that their two kids, ages eighteen and twenty, had not returned home at all to prepare for Monday's classes. On Monday morning, their stripped bodies were discovered in a sitting position, leaning up against a statue, holding hands.

Tuesday's sun dawned to reveal the murders of an elderly store owner and his wife. They had been closing up shop Monday night when they were taken by surprise by Shanice and her pal. They were skinned, eaten, and their bloody bones were left in the store aisle with the breakfast cereals and toaster pastries.

Wednesday brought the discovery of two young parents who had a set of twins, a boy and a girl aged less than one year. The children were screaming and crying in the early morning hours, which easily caught the attention of the neighbors in the small apartment complex. Police were called, and before 8:30 that morning, the bodies of the parents were discovered. They had been posed in their own bed as if they had been sleeping soundly, but it was obvious that their night consisted of nothing but horror.

Thursday and Friday came with the discovery of victims who, once again, were in no way related, nor were they found together. Both times, the victims consisted of one of each sex, and both times the bodies were found outside in different places. The only thing the four victims from these two days had in common was that all four were from Toledo; Greenville was bypassed entirely during these two nights.

On Saturday morning, a farmer and his wife were discovered by their adult daughter who had gone to their home to have breakfast. The wife was found in the living room, the husband on the front porch, and their collie, a dog named Trudy, was found with its throat slit in the middle of the gravel driveway.

But by Saturday none of it mattered because the entire area was in a state of sheer panic. Police didn't have to set a curfew because everyone was home way before dark with their doors and windows locked tight. The problem was that locks didn't seem to matter anymore and closed doors or staying inside were ineffective. Shanice simply didn't care; she was getting more and more dangerous and daring with each passing day.

CHAPTER 12

"Mavis, I think I know what's going on," Matt said, looking very serious.

"You do?"

Matt nodded. "Remember, right after Ben was killed, you said 'Could Shanice be a zombie?' Remember telling me about getting jumped by her and Candy in the alley? I mean, I wasn't around yet, but you've filled me in several times on the incident, right? You bit her... Shanice, I mean. That's what you said, and that's what I read in the copy of the police report you let me read. You bit her; you bit her on the cheek, and she walked away. I'll bet that bite made her like you, just like in the movies and books, Mav. I do think Shanice is a zombie."

His words put her into a state of shocked disbelief. A zombie? How could that be? Sure, in the movies that was the way it worked, but she had never considered it. The thought that a simple bite might turn someone into what she was made her skin crawl. Suddenly, she found herself thankful that she had gone all the way and eaten the people completely, leaving none alive.

None except Shanice Hall, one of the evilest people

she had ever met in her life.

Matt continued, almost talking to himself. "I'll bet she got into Greenville Psych, busted Candy out, and now she is going to turn her into a zombie if she hasn't already." He turned to her, sudden alarm all over his face. "I think maybe she wants revenge on you, Mavis. Revenge for getting her sent away, and for making her like you."

Mavis nodded. It made sense. No wonder it was Ben that died; she was now sure it was Shanice spying on them at Donnelly Park, and who knows how long she had been spying on them before that. Yes, Matt was right, and she was convinced. Shanice was back with a vengeance, and it was directed at her.

"What are we going to do, Matt?" Her voice was little more than a whisper, and it had an obvious shakiness to it.

∞

The sun was slowly going down behind the trees in the yards of each house for as far as their eye could see. Mavis and Matt sat on Jane's wrought iron bench, which was positioned near her slowly-fading flower bed, holding hands and staring silently at the purplish-gold beauty in the skies above.

There had been no bodies found for the last two days, though there had been two missing person reports filed, both announced on the local news. While Greenville was oblivious to the connection, Mavis and Matt were not. They knew that the "missing persons" were more than likely dead and that Shanice Hall was the culprit. But until the bodies were found, her secret was safe, and she knew it.

"I wish there were some way to stop her," Mavis said softly, breaking the silence. "Well, there is, but…"

Matt waited for a bit for her to finish before prodding her on. "But what?"

She shrugged. "Well, it would involve bringing me down to the station, I am starting to think that it would be worth it. It's the only way. I mean, how selfish am I to continue living any kind of life, even as a zombie, while she is out murdering people. It's my fault, Matt. And don't tell me that it isn't; we both understand the ripple effect, even if my being a zombie is an accident."

She looked away from him then, turning her eyes back to the sky. He didn't answer right away, and Mavis knew that he was getting her point. She also knew that it was his love and affection for her that drove him to keep the situation hidden. He didn't want to lose her, and while that made her feel good, it wasn't right.

"Look," he finally said. "I can't tell you what to do, but I know deep in my heart that you are right. I also know that turning yourself in just to stop her isn't going to change what has happened, or the outcome of the situation we are in. I should also add that I believe in my heart, that we can take care of this… somehow, someway, and still get on with our lives together."

Mavis looked down at their hands. Their fingers were gently laced together, and he was stroking her thumb with his own. "But the problem is that neither of us knows what to do about it, and things could go on forever this way, Matt."

"If you feel so strongly about this, then I encourage you to do what you want to do," he said, his voice cracking. "But I really wish you would give it a little time. Just a couple of weeks, I mean; we can set a date and make it the deadline."

She thought about his suggestion. "Okay. But what do we do in the meantime?"

"I've been thinking about that," Matt replied. "I'm going to be brutally honest here: the only way we are going to stop her is to catch her in the act of killing, or at least trying to. And that seems impossible, unless…"

"Unless what?"

Letting go of her hand, Matt turned to her fully. "Unless we have bait."

The two of them stared at each other, and after only seconds, they both began to smile. It might just work, Mavis thought. If she were able to simply live with a few more deaths, they would be able to lure her using "bait," but that bait would have to be her.

"So, that's easy," she said. "I'll just make myself as vulnerable as possible at every turn. Once she pokes her head out enough to attack me, you do her in."

Matt's smile faded. "You can't be the bait, Mavis."

A confused look came over her face. "I can't? Why not?"

"Don't you see? She doesn't want you dead; you already are! She wants you miserable." He paused and looked hard at her until she really got his point. "The only way to really hurt you is to hurt the ones you love.

The bait has to be one of your friends, your loved ones."

Mavis thought about it for a second. "I can't put any of my family or friends in danger, Matt."

"No, but I can," he said. "I will be the bait, and that's all there is to it."

"No…"

He put his hand quickly over her mouth to silence her. "Listen to me: it has to be this way. We won't give her the opportunity to get close enough to kill me. By the time we have the plan perfected, she won't stand a chance. Do you trust me?"

Mavis nodded, her mouth still covered.

"Then work with me here, okay?"

R.W.K. Clark

CHAPTER 13

Shawn Maher and Kim Coleman began unwrapping their burgers with great smiles and gusto, both of them eager to tear into their Sports Burger Mega Meals. Across from them in the booth, Mavis and Matt watched their own food on trays in front of them, as of yet untouched. It was so entertaining to observe the football player and his curvy girlfriend. If one didn't know better, they would think the healthy pair hadn't eaten in weeks.

"So, I'm glad we were finally able to make time to get together," Mavis began as she slowly unwrapped her single cheeseburger; the smell made her want to wrinkle her nose. Being a zombie didn't eliminate her from acting normal in public, and today, that meant ordering people food. "There has been so much going on, and we all really need to have an important talk."

Shawn was completely focused on his food, but Kim acknowledged her best friend's words with rapid nodding as she slurped a piece of dangling tomato into her juice-covered mouth.

"I know, I know," Kim finally replied. "What, with school, and the murders, and our future plans..." She gave Shawn a wink, then continued. "It's been hard to get together. So, what's so important?"

Matt gave Mavis a nudge with his elbow, signifying that she should be the one to talk, since he, too, was eating. Making sure to keep things appropriate for mealtime conversation, she went on to the heart of the matter.

"We've talked briefly, Kim, and we know that Shanice is back and she is up to no good." Mavis picked a bit at her bun and went on. "The fact is, it is Shanice and Candy that are murdering all over town, but we can't say anything to the cops because it would come back to me."

Kim looked confused. "Why?"

"Because I was the one that turned Shanice into a zombie, Kim," she whispered, leaning forward. "It's my fault... from when I bit her face in the alley last year."

Kim, who had just taken a fat bite of her burger, froze, the food hanging partway out of her mouth. Quickly, she dropped her sandwich onto the tray and grabbed a napkin, then spit the bite inside and wrapped it up. She paused for a moment, staring at her friend and thinking.

"So, I guess this is something you neglected to tell me," she finally said, her voice low. "I mean, we talked about Shanice stalking you and being back, but you said nothing to me about this, Mav. Nothing at all!"

Mavis smiled sadly. "I know, but Matt and I have only been really piecing it together ourselves. The fact is, she is one, like me, and she has turned Candy into one as well." All of the color drained from Kim's face, her food now forgotten, and she slumped back against the booth hard.

"So, what does this all mean?"

Now Matt took over. "What it means is very simple. She will hurt Mavis. Somehow, her whole intent is to get revenge on Mavis, for a couple of reasons. So, if we had told what we know, the cops would find out Mavis is… different. We would lose her, Kim, and she is not evil like that girl… not at all. We have to protect Mavis and the truth by dealing with this ourselves, with Shanice and Candy, in our own time and way."

"But what does this have to do with Shawn and me?" Kim asked, glancing at her boyfriend, who seemed completely oblivious to the entire conversation.

Mavis' face hardened for effect. "It means that she is going to hurt whoever she can, whenever she can, just to hurt me. She's pissed that I got her kicked out of school and locked up, and she's even more pissed that I bit her and, well, changed her life."

Kim groaned. "Where the hell are her mom and dad? Can't they just ground her or something?"

Matt rolled his eyes at Mavis and took over. "All of my research tells me they aren't around, and that she is posing as her mother to access the family funds. If I were a betting man, I would say she already killed them both, and their bodies are lying somewhere in another country or something. Who knows where they were living; Ben couldn't even figure that out."

"So, what is it you want me to do about all of this?

Or Shawn? We didn't do anything to her!"

Mavis reached across the table and took Kim gently by the hand. "You're my best friend, Kim, and she knows it. She won't hesitate to harm anyone I love, and I can promise you that. So, until we figure out how to get her either dead or detained without it coming back onto me, you have to be super safe."

Matt interjected. "Don't go anywhere alone, including staying home alone. According to 'legend' or whatever, zombie's heads have to be destroyed to kill them. It's the only way. So, carry a bat in Shawn's vehicle, and keep one next to your beds, both of you."

"Geez," Kim muttered. "This is crazy."

Mavis squeezed her hand. "Promise me."

Kim gave Shawn another look, but he was in his own world. Looking Mavis in the eye, she finally said, "Okay. I promise."

"And no talking about this to anyone," Matt added. "Swear?"

"We swear."

Kim pushed her food away, as did Matt and Mavis, but Shawn simply reached for his girlfriend's sandwich and kept eating. All three of them rolled their eyes, then laughed. It would be okay; Mavis was sure of it.

∞

Mavis spent the rest of the evening with Matt, outlining a very loose plan to get rid of Shanice Hall once and for all. They had the basics down on paper, including how to stay alive, but the details were all but non-existent. Matt realized they would need to include help for sure, based on what Mavis was able to do to the junior class all by herself. He knew they couldn't confront Shanice alone, as she was fast and strong, that was for sure, and they would also need weapons. They knew they would carry it out at night in an obvious place, like the Pointe or Donnelly Park. They knew they would involve Kim and Shawn if the two would agree, and only if they would be completely safe. They knew that they planned to bust Shanice's skull wide open and put her out of her misery.

What they didn't know was how long it was going to take to figure it all out, or what they were trying to figure out. So far, however, they had a foundation, and that was enough to make Mavis feel better. The thought of setting up Shanice and stopping her horrid rampage of destruction helped her focus better on her day to day life, even though the rampage itself was consistently spreading horror throughout Greenville, and even to all of Toledo. Both she and Matt knew that they had to continue to think and plan, and they were keeping Kim Coleman up to date on their progress, trusting her to share things with Shawn as they went. Kim was more than willing to participate, as was her boyfriend, even though she expressed her fears and apprehensions. She knew that if Shanice were to be stopped without bringing Mavis down with her, they were all going to have to push their fears aside and do what they had to do as a team.

Mavis leaned forward. "Matt, we really need to talk, seriously. I know you know we do. Are you just trying to not think about the reality of it?"

With a sigh, he turned all the way around to face her. "Yeah, I know, I know. I guess I'm just a little overwhelmed by all this. I mean, it's one thing to deal with you; you're a good person, not a bloodthirsty, hateful one who doesn't care who they hurt." Mavis felt a pain in her stomach. "Matt, are you… are you saying you don't want to deal with me anymore?"

Suddenly her eyes began to sting, and for the first time in a year, she felt the warmth of tears in them. It was an odd sensation, and one she immediately realized she didn't miss at all. Mavis wasn't sure why she was suddenly able to shed tears, but she believed that the thought of losing Matt, for any reason, was enough to get the job done.

It surprised Matt, too. He jumped up from the beanbag chair and rushed to her side. "No! No way, babe! I just got a little freaked out, but I'm in this with you all the way… I'm in this for the long haul, I promise you that!"

He took her in his arms and held her tight, and Mavis let her tears fall freely on his shoulder, wetting his t-shirt all the way through. When the tears stopped only a minute later, she looked up at him, searching his face and eyes.

"You mean it?" she asked. "I mean, I love you, and I don't want you to do anything that you don't want to do, Matt. I want you to be safe and happy."

He nodded and wiped her final tear away with his thumb. "I mean it, and I'm only happy when I'm with you. As for being safe, no one in Greenville, or anywhere else for that matter, is safe, and it isn't going to do any good for me to tuck tail and run and hide, now is it?"

Mavis shook her head. "I guess not."

"So, put those thoughts out of your mind, honey." Matt stroked her hair and smiled. "You're right, we need to put our heads together and figure out how to put a stop to this. But I have to be honest; I think the only way to stop this rampage is to put a stop to Shanice and Candy altogether, and there is only one way to do that and keep the focus off of you."

"Well," she replied thoughtfully, "we can't just go to her house, or even walk up to her on the street and bash her skull in, now can we? I mean, that's going to bring the attention on me too. I don't know what to do, but I can't live with the thought of her killing people every night."

"I don't think we have a choice." Matt was thinking hard too. "I mean, for one thing, stopping her would involve us following her around each and every night, and that's not feasible." After a moment, his face relaxed. "Here is my solution; we keep a close watch on the ones we care about, our friends and family. We make sure that they don't go out at night, and we accompany them every chance we get. We'll tell Kim and Shawn to stay away from isolated places... they'll get it. Then, we'll just let Shanice and Candy do whatever they are going to do, and eventually, they'll get themselves caught, I'm sure of it."

So, as the days went by slowly, they continued to work on their scheme, talking about it every chance they had, taking notes, and perfecting it as best as they could.

CHAPTER 14

Matt and Mavis stayed on task, however. They were busy spending a lot of time on the computer, searching for Shanice Hall. But it seemed that no matter how much looking they did, they found nothing. Both of them knew that her parents' names were Michael and Anita, but searches for them turned up nothing as well. They were just about to the point where they were going to give up when Matt just happened to be scanning the screen and came upon an "Aneta" Hall, who had recently purchased a loft in Toledo. It was just outside of Greenville; right on the edge of the suburb, as a matter of fact. As soon as his eye caught it, he knew he had found what they had been looking for.

"I found something, Mav," he said, his voice brimming with excitement. "I think I was spelling her mother's name wrong, but here is an Aneta, spelled with an 'e' instead of an 'i.' She just bought a loft residence here." He had clicked on the realtor site, which was actually part of the city's vital statistics department. It was then that he also saw that the same Aneta Hall had also purchased a new luxury sports car, and the salesman listed on the transaction was one Mark

Williams.

"Mark Williams." Matt paused and glanced at Mavis. "That was the name of the car salesman who was killed." He stopped and spun around in the desk chair so he could face Mavis. "So, do you think that this Aneta is here with Shanice? Maybe her father too?"

Mavis stared at him for a moment, then a sad look came over her face. "Do you really want to know what I think? Especially at this point, anyway?"

Matt nodded.

"I think Shanice started to change after I bit her," Mavis began. "I think her parents got her out of Greenville as fast as they could, and they took her far away to someplace where they thought she couldn't hurt anyone. And then, well, then I think she ate them both and is posing as her mom. That's what I think, Matthew."

Matt stared at her, the realization of the truth coming over him, but yet he clung to the hope that a teenaged girl wouldn't eat her own parents. "But, I mean, if her mom and dad took her away to help her not eat people, maybe they found a way to fix her and brought her back."

Mavis shook her head. "Matt, listen, you said yourself that the killings I did weren't murder. No matter how much that sounded like crap, I listened. I listened because it wasn't in my heart to kill anyone, and I knew that to be true. But Shanice got off on hurting others for as long as I knew her. Wouldn't becoming a zombie just make that trait in her heart worse than ever?"

He thought about what she said. "Yeah. I suppose you're right."

Mavis stood up and started to pace back and forth. "So, here's the gist of it: we have a mess on our hands, and it's up to us to solve it. Now, let's look at all the facts, from beginning to end."

She stopped long enough to dig a notebook out of her computer bag, then grabbed a pen off her desk and sat cross-legged on her bed. Uncapping the pen, she held it over the paper and looked up at Matt, who was waiting patiently for her to begin. It was obvious he was going to let her put this into perspective for him because she knew Shanice and Candy. Not well, granted, but she knew them better than he ever would.

"Okay. I had that run in with Candy and Shanice before homecoming last year. They jumped me in the alley on the way back from Flair's, and I bit Shanice on the cheek." She paused and began to write furiously. "Of course, we all know what happened: they got charged and went to Juvie... end of the story, one would think."

"One would think," Matt mumbled in agreement.

She looked up excitedly. "But I didn't think about the fact that I had bitten her, nor did I consider what the consequences of that might be because I had no idea what I was at that time. She must have started to show signs even while she was in Juvie, which would explain both of the girls having such a short stay for an assault crime!"

Matt nodded. "She started to get hungry. But they couldn't just let her out and not Candy. Shanice was the instigator, and everyone knew it. So, they do a little over a month, almost two, and they are released."

"And Shanice's parents relocate to Cleveland, which we know because that's what Ben Gordon learned last summer." She jotted down the bit about Cleveland and put Ben's name in parenthesis next to it, sadness coming over her as she did so. "Then, according to him as well, they disappeared off the face of the Earth. My guess is they just moved out of the country, maybe changing their names, maybe just living off savings and avoiding social media and the Internet altogether. It really doesn't matter, but they got it done. Now, all we have to do is find out if Shanice did her parents in or not."

"How are we going to do that?" Matt asked, but she could tell his wheels were turning. "We know that Mr. Hall's name is nowhere on the title to the new loft... only Aneta's, and there is no record of Shanice enrolling in school or getting a job... nothing."

"That's precisely why I believe she is pretending to be her mother." She thought for a minute. "So, we have the loft address, and Shanice hasn't had a problem stalking me out, so let's do the same."

Matt sat forward; now she was speaking his language. "When do we start?"

Mavis shrugged and tossed the notebook onto the bed beside her. "I don't see why we shouldn't begin tonight."

CHAPTER 15

The street outside the loft building was well lit, and not surprisingly, the neighborhood was clean and quiet. Mavis knew that Shanice had been brought up with a silver spoon in her mouth, so whether her mother was actually with her, or Shanice was posing as the woman, really didn't matter. The girl was going to choose to have nice things regardless of the particulars of the situation. If she was posing as Aneta Hall, she likely had unlimited funds backing the decisions she made... hence the luxury sports car, as well.

The loft was located inside a building that was, at one time, zoned for industrial use. Mavis seemed to recall that it had been some kind of factory when she was a young girl but also remembered that it was remodeled into living space not five years ago. Her father and mother had chatted over it at length on a number of occasions, oohing and aahing over the high prices of the four large, spacious units inside. It was high-end, and even in the darkness, it looked the part.

The pair were in Matt's old black car. It was one of two he owned, but it was not his first choice to drive. Typically, when he wasn't with Mavis in the convertible, he was tooling around in a beat-up truck, claiming outlandish gas mileage and little to no consideration for what other people thought. The truck was gray because it had primer applied prior to a paint job he never got around to. Tonight, Matt had opted for the car for a couple of reasons: one, if Shanice had been stalking him as well, she would never have seen this car. It was not only easy to hide the black beast in the shadows, but also it was roomy enough to duck down in if Shanice or Candy were to suddenly appear. In the truck or the convertible, they would have been dead in the water, exposed for the taking.

But here it was, 9:30 at night, and they were parked on the block that sat kitty-corner from the loft building. The entire place was in full view, but they were strategically parked, so they were just out of place, making the existence of the car, and the two teens inside, easy to miss for someone on a mission.

Mavis and Matt both agreed that it was highly likely for Shanice and Candy to leave at some point in the near future. The reason for this thinking was the fact that the flesh-eater murders of the car salesman and Ben Gordon took place at night. Shanice was killing without regard, but she wasn't stupid enough to do it in broad daylight. While Mavis took her primary nourishment in the mornings, with snacks she saved throughout the day, she also ate regular food. This kept her body feeling full, even if her indulgences weren't satisfied. Shanice was doing things the opposite way: eating at night, and more than likely saving little snacks, too. But now she was providing for two and would be until Candy learned to stand on her own two feet if she was at all capable of that.

Yes, they would be going out for a bite to eat anytime.

While the pair waited, they snacked on corn chips and drank sodas. Mavis had a big wad of vapor rub under her nose so being cooped up with Matt wouldn't become a temptation. While they munched and waited, she thought about the fact that Matt really wasn't her concern. If for some reason, Shanice noticed them sitting there and decided to investigate, Shanice would see Matt as fresh meat. There would be only one way to save him: she would have to do it herself; she would have to fight them off of him to the death.

Mavis had no problem doing that at all.

From 9:30 to 10:30, they chatted lightly, in low voices, as though the entire neighborhood could hear them. There was next to no traffic with only two cars passing by them during the entire hour. Without worry, they simply sat low and kept their eyes peeled.

But once 10:30 arrived, Mavis started to get a little nervous. She had told her mother that Matt was taking her for burgers, and then they were going to take a quiet drive before returning home so they could "talk." Jane and Todd were very loose and trusting when it came to their daughter, but they did expect her in bed by 11:30, midnight being the very latest.

But, even in the midst of her anxiety, as the minutes ticked slowly by, Mavis began to forget about her parents. What would they say, really? She had done nothing, throughout the short span of her life, to make her parents ever question her word. Consequently, she had earned their trust and their friendship. She had two very good friends and trustworthy guides on the trip through life. No, she wouldn't worry; instead, she would focus on the task at hand and see to it that things were taken care of properly… with the help of Matt, of course.

So, they sat. They chatted in whispers, and they giggled when the jokes were right, and at 10:54, to be precise, the lower garage door on the condo building where "Aneta" Hall's loft was opened. Both Mavis and Matthew froze as they stared at the sight they never expected to see.

Slowly, but surely, a silver luxury sports coupe pulled slowly from the underground garage. There were two people in the front seats, and from what the pair could see, both were female, but no other discernable figures could be made out. It stopped at the end of the drive, then paused just long enough to look both ways before taking a quick right turn into the night.

Mavis turned to Matt, her eyes wide. "That was them, Matt."

"I know." His voice was low, but he was on top of things. He put the car gently into gear and then slowly pulled forward, without the headlights on, as he made his way forward into the night behind the two people Mavis believed to be Shanice Hall and Candy Wilkes.

They pulled directly into the sparse traffic behind

the sports car, keeping several good yards between the two vehicles. The car kept a steady trek, though it did seem to know exactly where it was going. Mavis' eyes were so peeled that she thought they would pop out of her head; Matt, on the other hand, was focused on simply keeping up with the car ahead of him.

"What should I do?" he asked nervously, especially for someone who seemed to be a zombie specialist.

Mavis continued to stare. "I guess you keep following them but keep your distance. I gotta tell you, I think they're going to feed someplace. I mean, it's only logical, don't you think?"

Matt made a noise of agreement, but it was definitely filled with apprehension. Mavis, on the other hand, was positive about what was going on: they were looking for dinner, and if her instincts were correct, little Miss Shanice was already on the rampage for the meal she had in mind.

"Listen, Matt," she said in a steady voice, "we have to keep up from way behind. There is one reason that the two of them are cruising right now: they're hungry. I swear to you, no matter where they go, we can stop a murder right now. Are you willing to be grounded? I am!!"

Matt chuckled. "Grounded, huh? Well, heck yeah. Let's go get ourselves grounded, why don't we!"

Mavis failed to catch the sarcasm in his voice; all it seemed she could hear was the sound of the sports car's tires as they softly peeled on the concrete of the avenue. As far as smells, her nose seemed to be consumed with the cloying scent of vapor rub and the breezy aroma from the flesh of the two individuals driving in front of them. Maybe it was the circumstances surrounding the situation, but it almost seemed like the smell of the two girls was getting stronger by the second.

They smelled simply rotten.

Mavis was completely entranced by the luxury sports car, though it definitely wasn't the car that had her rapt, almost hypnotized, attention. It was that rotten flesh smell that seemed to seep through the jelly under her nose. If that smell was coming off of Shanice Hall and Candy Wilkes, did it come off her, too? Oh, yuck, was that what she smelled like all the time... around other people? She was beside herself with panic over it.

Now the coupe took a right, then a quick left, before starting up a long, winding hill that led to Harbin's Pointe, another popular make-out place among the kids of Greenville.

"I think they're going to the Pointe," Matt muttered, "which is weird, considering how late it is, and the fact that it's a school night." He glanced over at Mavis, only to see her staring, open-mouthed and in confusion, at the car ahead. "Mavis, did you hear me? What's wrong with you?"

She turned to him slowly, but at first, her expression didn't change. After a moment of distant staring, she said to him in a voice tinged with horror, "I can smell them, Matt. Even through the vapor rub, I can, and it smells like straight-up death. Is that what I smell like, Matt? Do I smell like a rotting body?"

He glanced over at her, one eyebrow raised, then turned his attention back to the road, so he didn't get the car too close. "No, Mavis. That isn't how you smell, not to me, anyway. Maybe you should ask someone else, like Kim or your mom, but right now we have to worry about the task at hand. There isn't another outlet from the Pointe, is there? Other than this one, I mean?"

Mavis shook her head back and forth to help her regain her focus. "No, this is the only road out. If they intend to kill someone up here, they won't do it with us behind them. Turn into that driveway up there and kill the lights, Matt."

He immediately did as she directed. Slowly, with no headlights, he turned the car around on the steep snake-like drive until it was facing the road again. With the engine still running, he turned to Mavis with patient expectation.

"Good, perfect," she said, as if on cue. "We'll sit here for like, I don't know, five or ten minutes. Maybe five is better; we don't want to give them time to actually kill anyone if they find anyone to eat." Mavis absently reached into her purse and pulled out her vapor rub, smearing more of it liberally under her nose until it was literally glistening in the dashboard lights. "Not only do I not want to smell the stinky girls, but I also don't want to be tempted to join them if they happen to be having a meal when we arrive."

Matt turned to her. "Look, I don't care what they're doing when we go up there, but I think it would be best if I stay in the car and lock the doors. Nothing personal,

Sweets. I just want to live through this. I mean, I brought a baseball bat to bash their heads in if I have to, but I don't want to run the risk of needing to bash your head in."

"Sounds good to me," she replied as she put the jar of rub back into her bag. "I say we give it a couple more minutes, then head up. Like I said, I don't want to give them too much time to do damage."

"But, if there was no one up there, wouldn't they have been on their way back down by now?" Matt asked.

Mavis felt a pang of panic with the realization that he was right. "Yep. Forget waiting; let's go now."

Matt put the lights on and the car into gear before pulling out of the driveway and back onto the winding road. They crept along this time, doing no more than twenty miles per hour; Matt was obviously nervous about the entire situation. Mavis could tell because when they got to the main entrance to the gravel area where everyone parked, he stopped and killed the lights once again.

But whether the lights were on or off didn't matter. The moonlight was shining brightly, and in it were the clear forms of both Shanice and Candy. They were kneeling over what could only be a pair of bodies, their faces buried in the midsections of those they were eating. A car sat parked with both driver and passenger door open, and the interior light of the vehicle was shining brightly, making it even easier for the pair to see what was taking place.

In their feeding frenzy, neither Shanice nor Candy was aware of the presence of Mavis or Matt. They were so oblivious to all that was going on around them that it would have been simple to just sneak up on them and bash both of their brains in right then and there. This was a point Matt felt extremely comfortable voicing.

"I'm just going to sneak up and smash them." He was already reaching into the back for his bat, but Mavis stopped him right away, putting her hand on his arm.

"Matthew, even if you managed to get one of them, the other would be on you faster than lightning," she whispered. "You'd be no more than a take-out meal to the survivor. I have to go; you stay here and lock the doors, just like you said. I'm going to go out there and confront them; you just hold on to that bat just in case. Remember, we can't get anywhere near those dead bodies, or we'll both be dragged into a brand-new murder investigation."

He only nodded, placing the bat across his lap and getting a firm grip on it. Mavis leaned over and planted a kiss firmly on his lips, then carefully and quietly opened the door to the car, which happened to have a dome light that didn't work at all, fortunately. Matt looked like he might be sick.

"Please be careful," he whispered. "It will be two on one."

Mavis nodded. "I know, but I'm not afraid, and the fact that I'm one of the good guys is in my favor. Just lock the doors, and if you see me coming, get mine unlocked fast."

Without another word, she slipped out of the car and shut the door lightly enough that it only emitted a soft "cluck" sound. Kneeling down next to the door, she peered through an opening in a clump of bushes to see if the girls had heard the noise, but they didn't even flinch. Mavis took a deep breath, stood up, and began to take long strides in their direction, a fierceness in her heart and fury on her mind.

It was time for the first face to face showdown between her and her flesh-eating tormentors, the very tormentors she had created.

CHAPTER 16

"Hey!" she shouted. "Hey, you! Both of you! Still a couple of bullies, huh? Can't even get being a freaking zombie in the real world right, can you, you couple of losers?"

Immediately, both Shanice and Candy looked up from their feasting, almost in unison. Between the moonlight and the dome light from the dead couple's car, Mavis could make out their blood-covered faces clearly. Yes, it was indeed Shanice Hall and Candy Wilkes, and they were smiling with pleasure.

With her meal forgotten, Shanice slowly stood, her smile growing. "Well, well, well, look who came to visit, Candy. Mavis herself, mother of all the zombies. Hi, Mavis; did you come just to say 'hi,' or were you planning on staying for dinner?"

She began to cackle at her own joke, as did Candy, but it took the dimmer Miss Wilkes a bit more time to catch the sarcasm. Slowly, Candy began to rise as well, but not with the grace that Shanice had shown; she almost fell back down twice.

"I hope it isn't for dinner," Candy added. "I don't think we have enough for three."

The two of them began to slowly close the gap between themselves and Mavis, but she didn't move a muscle. She felt no fear at all, only the rage of someone who had chosen to do right, regardless of her circumstances, yet watched as others like her reveled in their choice to do the opposite.

"You are such a piece of crap," she began, standing her ground and keeping her eyes on Shanice. "You thrive on the pain and suffering of others."

Candy stopped, a confused look on her face as if Mavis' words were simply too much to handle. But Shanice's smile grew, and she took another step toward Mavis. A long stringer of flesh dangled from her teeth which, along with her blood-soaked face, made Mavis feel deep repulsion.

Shanice got about five feet from Mavis and asked, "Don't you do the same? It's one thing to be a bully and a taker; it's another thing to lie and pretend that it isn't what you are. You're nothing more than a hypocrite who does the same. Heck, Mav, you made me who I am!"

"Regretfully so," she replied. "And as a matter of fact, I don't do what you do. I have chosen to take the safer route, the route that keeps people from dying. But you would have been a killer with or without that bite I gave you."

Shanice maintained her smile while she thought about what Mavis said. "You're right: I hate people! I don't consider one of them… any of them, to be above me, or even on the same level as I am. Maybe I would have been a killer without the bite, but maybe not. I can tell you this, though. I would definitely make each and every person who ever crossed my path miserable, just like I am about to do to you!"

Without any warning, Shanice Hall broke into a full run, bum-rushing Mavis and knocking her to the ground. The girl's arms were swinging at Mavis in windmill fashion, but Mavis staved off each and every blow like deflecting bullets. At one point she caught a quick glance at Candy, who had made her way back to the body on the ground and was pigging out again.

When Mavis had enough of the silly games Shanice was miserably trying to dish out, she drew her knees to her chest, planted her feet firmly on Shanice's chest, and shoved her backward. The girl flew through the air and landed on her back with a loud "oof," the wind knocked out of her but good. Mavis scrambled to her feet and planted them firmly on the ground, standing with her hands on her hips directly over the gasping Shanice. A quick glance to her right told her that Candy was lost in the infatuation of flesh and blood eating, and she posed no threat to the current situation. Once she was satisfied that she was safe from the double-threat, Mavis looked down at Shanice and sneered.

"Now, let's get this perfectly clear, Shanice Hall," she began. "I didn't want to go through this zombie thing any more than anyone else; it happened quite by accident, and I had no idea when I bit you that this would be the result. You attacked me, and I was defending myself. But if you think for five seconds that you are going to come back to Greenville and victimize me, or my family or friends, you have another think coming. I know what you did, Shanice; I know that you killed Ben Gordon, and for that, I will forever hate you, but not enough to let you destroy my life or my future plans. So take your murderous corpse back where you came from, and take your human blood-sucking friend with you."

Shanice gave a cough and a gasp before slowly pushing herself up into a sitting position. "I don't have to go anywhere. Don't you see, little Miss Mavis Harvey? I have a vendetta. First, you bit me and ruined my life; I was forced to eat my way through Tuscany, ending with my own parents!"

"You didn't care about them anyway," Mavis shot back. "You don't care about anything or anyone but yourself, including your dimwitted little minion over there."

Candy looked up from a handful of kidney. "Huh?"

Mavis groaned. "I could care less about your need for revenge. I'm warning you now, if you harm another person in Greenville, or if you think for a second you are going to lay this crap on me, I'm going to let my boyfriend splatter what's left of your rotten brain all over the garage of your new loft, you got me?"

Now Shanice got to her feet. "Make your threats. But I have to ask, what are you going to do about the situation at hand? Run to the cops?"

"You bet your stinky zombie corpse," Mavis growled. "I know where you live, and I'll turn you in so fast your head will spin. But… if you decide right now to walk away and let this whole thing go, and take Candy with you, I'll report a couple of dead bodies anonymously, and we can forget the last year… capiche?"

"Huh?" Candy repeated upon hearing her name for the second time.

"Nothing, Candy!" Both girls said in stereo. Candy shrugged and went back to eating, a handful of intestine.

Shanice turned back to Mavis. "All I'm going to say is fine… for now." She turned to Candy and said, "Grab what you can and let's get out of here… fast. The cops are coming, Candy."

"But… but… but I'm not done!" the girl whined.

Shanice growled. "Now!"

With intestines dangling from her hands, the girl ran to the luxury sports car and got inside, slamming the door behind her. Shanice turned back to Mavis as she began to back toward her car. She was still smiling, and still nodding in a very sinister way.

"This is far from over, Harvey," she sneered. "I'll take the current deal on the table, but this has nothing to do with the future… or what it holds for you and me. There will be a showdown, and I will take control of Greenville for my purposes, once and for all."

Shanice reached her car, jumped inside, and spun out in a donut before heading out of the Pointe gravel lot, driving past the car and Matt as if she didn't see or smell hide nor hair of him.

Mavis walked over to the two dead corpses lying on

the dirty ground. Their eyes were wide open with surprise, but other than that, most of their faces were gone. She didn't even hear Matt's footsteps as he approached her; she was filled with rage and grief and every other undesirable emotion.

"Are you okay?" he asked softly.

Mavis shrugged, keeping her eyes on the dead kids, who were the next Greenville victims. "I am for now, but no one I care about is. Do you have your cell? We need to call the police."

"What are we going to tell them?" he asked.

Mavis shook her head in disgust and turned to him. "We came up to make out and found this. A car, peeled out as soon as we got here. We can't tell them it was Shanice and Candy, or they're going to arrest them and realize what they are. As sure as my name is Mavis Harvey, they'll tell the cops that I'm a zombie too. We have to make it look like we came upon this situation without any knowledge of what really happened. You go ahead and make the call, Matt, but hide your bat in the car's trunk first."

He did as she said, and as he spoke with the 911 operator, Mavis simply stared at the carnage before her. With a broken heart, she realized that she was the catalyst behind all of this. It didn't matter that Shanice was pure evil; none of this would have happened if not for that ill-fated bite on that fall day a year ago.

She wanted to fall to her knees and weep, but Mavis knew that no tears would come, no matter how hard she tried.

CHAPTER 17

Mavis lay on her bed, staring at the ceiling and replaying the previous night's incident over and over in her mind. It was nearly 10:30 in the morning and classes at Westside had been canceled due to the teen murders at Harbin's Pointe, so she had nothing to do but think and re-think. Her stomach was growling like crazy; the situation from the night before had also hindered Matt's ability to bring something for her to eat. At that very moment he was at Flair Foods buying raw liver for her, and though she had quickly tired of the replacement food, she could hardly wait for him to return.

They had been at the police station until one in the morning, answering questions and telling their side of the story over and over. Only one thing had the cops a bit wary: Mavis had blood on her clothing. Not a lot of blood, but enough that she had to explain it, which she did by saying she had knelt down to try and save one of the victims that she thought was still alive. The cops ended up buying it because it wasn't a large amount. Only she and Matt knew that the blood transfer occurred when Shanice charged at her and knocked her to the ground.

Both of them had stuck to the story perfectly, telling it from their own perspectives and in their own words. They had pulled up to the Pointe for a little hugging and kissing, and as soon as they entered the gravel lot, a small, newer car (Matt claimed he thought was silver, while Mavis told the police she had no idea of its make or model) revved up its engine and sped past them. It was then that they noticed the car with the open door and the dome light on, and immediately after that, they stumbled upon the two dead kids.

Their parents were called to come to the station, and just as a matter of procedure, they had to fill out reports by hand, recalling the story yet again. By the time the Harvey and Morgan families were able to leave the police station and head for home, they were all exhausted and shook up. It didn't help that, on the way home, Mavis had to listen to her mother go on and on about some cannibalistic serial killer running loose in Greenville. Mavis wanted to correct her and tell her there were two, but she kept her lips sealed and tolerated her mother's insane concern.

But now, as she lay there on her bed recalling all of it, she knew that her mother's concerns were anything but insane. In fact, they were so sane that it was chilling. Mavis wasn't as worried so much about "serial killers" and such, because she knew what Shanice was up to. It involved getting back at her in a way that would ruin her life if it didn't end it.

The thing bothering her the most, even more than the fact that Shanice and her goofy sidekick were running around killing and eating people, was the fact that the girl had Mavis and her loved ones in her sights. The killing was for sustenance, and Mavis knew that for a fact, from painful experience. It was the zombie's nature, she had learned, to do those things. It was only because of the person she was inside that she didn't continue to do it herself. That and Matt, of course. But Shanice was evil to the core, and it didn't bother her a bit to tear the life out of others. Whatever she had planned to hurt Mavis, it wasn't going to end well if Mavis just sat back and let it happen. Something had to be done to stop all of this, but what?

Right then a light knock came on her bedroom door, jerking her out of her own thoughts. "Yeah?"

The knob turned and in walked Matt with a plastic grocery bag from Flair's. "Sorry it took me so long," he greeted as he closed and locked the door behind him. "It seemed like everybody and their brother wanted to talk to me about last night. Since the bodies were identified as Bobby Carl and Leslie McCann, the whole town is in an uproar, and everyone thought I had details and juicy tidbits. I'm sure glad they canceled classes today. Could you imagine?"

Leslie McCann was likely the main reason for the uproar, Mavis knew. Her father was a councilman for Greenville, and he also owned a big chain of furniture stores, making him one of the richest men in the area as well. Bobby Carl was a senior who played football, so he was going to be grieved just for that reason alone by the public.

"It's just a bit much, and seeing Bobby and Leslie all torn up and dead like that... I just can't seem to get the picture out of my mind, much less than think straight about anything else."

Mavis began recapping the experience at Harbin's Pointe and the killings of Bobby and Leslie, "I mean, we didn't help them, we caught them in the act. We know now they killed Detective Gordon and all when we caught them at the point they were both in the middle of... the middle of... well, you know." Shanice killed Ben to hurt Mavis. Somehow, she put it together that the two had become close, and it didn't hurt that he was the one in charge of putting Candy in the nut house.

Matt was afraid of what might happen if he traveled alone at night, and so were his parents, which made life more difficult for all of them. Only Mavis and Matt really knew the true danger. If either Mr. and Mrs. Harvey or the Morgans got wind of it, both she and Matt would be kept under lock and key, powerless to stop Shanice and her schemes. Even though it was terribly dangerous to do so, both of them, and Kim and Shawn knew they had to keep the details under wraps, or Shanice may never be caught.

"I just know that everyone's parents are sick to death over it all," she mumbled as she spread a black garbage bag on the floor and started to eat her liver. "Did my mom ask what was in the bag?"

Matt shook his head and plopped down in the beanbag chair. "I didn't see her. Her car is in the drive, but she didn't answer the bell. I just let myself in. I hollered her name a couple of times; didn't you hear me?"

Mavis swallowed a big wad of liver while a bit of watery blood trickled down her chin, which she gave a wipe with the back of her hand. "I was pretty lost in thought, believe me. Thanks for picking this up for me."

"I love ya, girl!"

After giving him a wink she tore off another huge bite, and while she finished her food, Matt turned on the TV and began to surf the channels. They sat in silence, watching each channel he landed on, as she ate the rest of her liver. When she was done, and the mess was cleaned up and bagged up, Mavis plopped down on the bed and waited for Matt to realize she was waiting patiently for his attention. It didn't take long for him to feel her eyes on him.

"What?"

Mavis' eyes immediately went wide, and she jumped up from the bed like a shot. "Matt, my mom! You said you didn't see her, and she didn't answer when you called!"

The pair took off out of the bedroom in a panic, with Mavis screaming for Jane the whole way down the hall. No Jane in her bedroom, and no Jane in the living room or kitchen. They both ran out the front door, and just as Matt said, Jane's car sat in the driveway.

Mavis turned to Matt, horror all over her face. "I swear, Matthew if she hurt my mother I'll bash her head in myself."

Matt's eyes lit up, and he smiled. "The backyard, Mavis. I'll bet she's in the backyard."

They both ran through the house, and before they even got to the sliding glass door in the kitchen, Mavis could see Jane, kneeling in her flower bed, yanking weeds and wiping the sweat off her brow. She flung the door open and ran outside.

"Mother! You scared me to death!"

Jane was nearly startled out of her skin by the sound of her daughter's voice. "Oh, Mavis! Talk about scaring people! What's the matter with you?"

Mavis ran to Jane and threw her arms around the woman's neck, practically squeezing the life out of her. Jane just stood there, staring at Matt over her daughter's shoulder, a confused look on her face. Her gloved hands were held straight out to keep from getting dirt all over Mavis.

After a minute Mavis let her go. "Don't you know there's a homicidal maniac running around eating people? I think everyone in the family should tell people where they are going and what they are doing at all times, at least until this person is caught. We couldn't find you! We thought you were in trouble!"

Understanding came over her mother's face. "You're right, dear. I'm sorry. I didn't even think, and I should have. Especially after what you two kids went through last night."

"Fine. I forgive you, but you scared me to death." Mavis took a deep breath and smiled. "So, we're in agreement? We report to each other until the killer is caught?"

"Agreed," Jane replied. "Now, can I get back to my flower bed, please?"

The kids left her to her work and made their way into the house. "Next step," Mavis said as they walked, "is to call Kim."

CHAPTER 18

That evening, Shanice Hall and Candy Wilkes sat in a rented minivan on a gravel road running alongside the freeway. Cars passed like lightning, to and fro, but they were watching the mouth of the road they were on. They were waiting for some random chump to come help them with a make-believe flat tire, just like Ben Gordon had. That way they could have their dinner.

When it came to Mavis, Shanice had plans brewing, but she wasn't ready to talk to Candy about them yet. She wasn't surprised that the cops hadn't come to arrest them over eating those kids, though that would endanger Mavis, too. Shanice knew she had leverage, and her little schemes were taking form.

Before it was over, she would destroy Mavis' life but good.

For now, however, the main priority was food. Shanice had been finding out rather quickly that Candy's transformation had taken her from the mild form of mentally dull that she once had been to a whole new low of stupid. She had tunnel vision when it came to eating, and even though Shanice had explained about exercising a bit of self-control for the sake of the goal, and even though Candy understood that getting back at Mavis was to be the end result, she was easily distracted by her insatiable hunger. It made things very difficult for Shanice. Even though Candy was her best friend and long-time lackey, Shanice was beginning to seriously regret busting her out of the institution and making her part of the plan.

While her thoughts raced, Shanice continually kept her eyes on the mouth of the gravel road, waiting for any sign of headlights that would give them hope for nourishment. But Candy, on the other hand, was staring intently out the passenger side window at the traffic on the freeway. In the last half-hour, it had ebbed significantly; it was getting later. Shanice was just about to give up and try to find another gravel road when suddenly Candy shouted out.

"Look!" she yelled. "It's her! That's Mavis, across the freeway by the broken down car!"

This caught Shanice's attention immediately. Turning toward the freeway, she saw that a car had indeed pulled off to the side of the far shoulder, and a female with long black hair had gotten out and was making her way to the trunk of the brown sedan. The girl was alone.

Shanice squinted. "No, Candy. She doesn't smell right."

The windows were down, and the scent wafting across the freeway from the female wasn't that of the rot that zombies exuded, the smell that humans seemed to miss with enough perfume and cologne. No, it was definitely someone else.

"It's not her," Shanice insisted. "And besides, she's on the other side of the freeway. Too dangerous."

"No," Candy said angrily. "It's her, and I'm going to be the one to take her down. We'll feast on that little vixen tonight, and this will all be done once and for all."

Before Shanice could even comprehend what was happening, Candy was out of the minivan and running full-speed, across the gravel, through the grassy median, and straight out into the freeway and oncoming traffic.

"Candy, no!"

But it was too late. What happened next took place so fast, but it was like slow-motion. A semi-truck plowed into Candy Wilkes head on. In only seconds, the girl was splattered all over the road, and chaos on the freeway broke out just as fast.

Shanice had seen it all, and she had seen it clearly. Candy's body wasn't just torn limb from limb, but her head had splattered like an overripe melon. Even her brains, or what was left of it, had taken flight and hit the concrete, splattering everywhere.

Candy Wilkes was history, and it happened in the blink of an eye.

Without turning on the minivan's headlamps, Shanice got out of there fast. She would go directly home and eat leftovers; she had no choice now. Even though she felt bad, it was for the best, and she knew it. Shanice was worried they would do an autopsy, and they would see that Candy wasn't normal… she was undead. Either way, Candy would get the blame for all the murders, plain and simple. Hopefully, they won't do an autopsy, she thought to herself.

Shanice steered the minivan toward home, pushing the pain away and humming with cheer. This was good, the death of her friend. Hell, she was a burden anyway. Now she could plan a new army or even a couple more minions that would do. She would make sure they were smart and evil, just like her. Together, they would wage war on Mavis with success, not stumbles and bumps and burdens.

Now she could really start to kick things into proper motion.

CHAPTER 19

News of the death of Candy Wilkes spread like wildfire throughout the suburb of Greenville and the surrounding area. Of course, her parents were the first to be notified, but it didn't take long for the rest of the town to get the word around at all. It certainly took only seconds for rumors of abnormalities in her body, observed first by emergency responders, to hit the public's ears as well.

After all, it seemed that Miss Candy Wilkes was already dead when she was splattered all over the highway by that truck. No one, including the coroner, could make sense of it. The one question that went unanswered was how did the dead body of Candy Wilkes end up on the highway? The coroner did tie together two loose ends that were very important: her teeth patterns matched many of those found on the bones of Leslie McCann, not to mention that tiny particles of human flesh were found between her teeth. By the time the coroner was able to give an official report, he was willing to testify that Candace Wilkes was the one who had been terrorizing Greenville for the past year.

It looked like Ben Gordon had been right all along, and now the suburb of Toledo was breathing a sigh of relief.

Shanice was thrilled. Now she could set about taking the next step in her ever-expanding plan to destroy Mavis.

Mavis, however, was devastated. Now it seemed that any reference to Shanice Hall was going to be looked upon as madness. Mavis knew the death of Candy, accidental or otherwise, was not the end of the situation. It was only the beginning. Neither she nor Matt Morgan could even begin to guess what the horrible Shanice had up her sleeve next. All they were willing to bet on was that she was a busy girl indeed, and the death of Candy did nothing but clear the path for her terrible plans.

Had the death been an accident? Had it been suicide? Or was it an ingenious and manipulative play on Shanice's part to rid herself of the friend who, as a zombie, had become nothing more than dangerous, stupid baggage? Only time would tell.

The entire suburb was buzzing with it all. The only exception was Matt and Mavis, who were now more concerned than ever. The nightly killings were not going to stop, they knew. The only thing that was going to change was the outright sloppiness of Shanice leaving bodies lying around. She was likely going to keep the focus off herself, after all, she was on a mission.

On the evening after Candy was killed, everything that Matt and Mavis suspected about Shanice and her parents began to come to light.

They were sitting with Jane and Todd, watching the evening world news program that Todd looked forward to so much. With full bellies from their dinner (fried chicken with the works, which Mavis faked her way through; she had eaten cow heart earlier, thanks to Matt pulling a shift the evening before), they sat in front of the television and got caught up on everything politics, scandal, and pre-end-of-the-world.

But then, during the very last segment, there was breaking news from Tuscany, Italy. Two people were found dead, apparently with the flesh either torn or eaten, from their bodies, leaving nothing more than scraps and bones. They were confirmed to be male and female, late-thirties, and they had been there for some time. But that was only the beginning.

Next, the anchorman explained that the identities of the bodies were a point of confusion. The home they were found in was owned by a married couple by the names of Dr. Philip Benini and his wife, Mona. They had immigrated with their seventeen-year-old daughter Gretchen only eight short months ago. Initially, no family could be found to notify, but after less than a day after they had been discovered, Italian governing authorities were able to determine that the bodies really belonged to Dr. Michael Hall and his wife, Aneta, American citizens. Unfortunately, their daughter, whose real name was Shanice, was missing, and foul play was suspected. Italian authorities believed that Shanice was being held by criminals who were holding her for access to her parents' significant assets. Photos of Shanice were splayed across the screen, along with warnings that, if she was spotted, either in Italy or the States, citizens should not try to intervene, but should contact authorities immediately.

As soon as the piece was over, Todd turned off the set, and the four of them sat in silence. After several moments, Todd turned to Mavis and Matt, a very serious and concerned look on his face. Both of the kids braced themselves; they had to answer any questions, but it was vital that they didn't give away too much.

"Now we know for sure she is here, isn't she?" He asked. "Ben wasn't joking around, and she did this to her parents, she helped Candy escape, and she is directly involved in these murders. Tell me the truth, Mavis."

Mavis gave a glance to Matt as if to say, 'What should I do?' But Matt just stared at her with trust; she would say the right thing to spare her parents' sanity regarding her state. She would be fine.

"Well… yes, Ben was right. She is here, as you know from the prank call he suspected she made to me." In an effort to face both of her parents, she turned her body away from Matt. "The truth is, she is sort of… out to get me, I guess, like we discussed. But I can't really see her eating her own parents, Dad, no matter how black her heart is."

The lie came off her lips easily, and it made her feel guilty. But she had her parents to consider, so she pushed the feeling away. Holding their stares, she waited for Jane and Todd's next question.

Jane spoke this time, suspicion and doubt in her

voice. "Well, Mavis Jean, I'm going to just spit it out. I find it highly questionable that there have been these… cannibal murders, two of which you and Matthew witnessed, here in Greenville and Toledo. Now we hear that two people identified as this little heathen's parents were killed the same way. Now Candy is dead, and the blame falls on her, but all of us know that Candy was in Greenville psych at the time the Halls were murdered. So, I guess I feel like that leaves only one person: the poor, kidnapped little orphan and bully, Shanice Hall."

Mavis sat back and looked at Matt again, but he just shrugged and sighed, forcing Mavis to respond on her own once again.

"Yes, I have to say that's a weird… coincidence, yes." She paused to think her next words through. "Um, as a matter of fact, it seems pretty obvious that she is probably involved somehow."

Todd got to his feet in a huff. "Pretty obvious? Are you blind? Is this the type of thing we, as a family with loved ones, have to worry about? Some enemy from your junior year coming to eat one, or all, of us?" He plopped down in his chair again and put his hand to his forehead, eyes closed, as if a headache were coming on.

Calmly and gently, Jane asked, "Is there something the two of you aren't telling us?"

Finally, Matt came to the rescue. "I guess we failed to mention that when Shanice called Mavis, she did sort of threaten with hurting her loved ones. None of us expected this, though. But I know it's safe to say she had something to do with Ben's death… I mean, considering the way he died."

"You think?" Todd's voice was filled with sarcasm. He opened his eyes and looked at both of the kids. "Have you told the police your suspicions?"

"No…" Mavis mumbled.

Jane asked, "Why not?"

"For a lot of reasons, ma'am," Matt said. "First, we don't know where she is or anything. She is certainly not using her real name, or that would be a dead giveaway, and she would then be easy to find. For another, we're not positive it is her."

"You mean to tell me you witnessed a murder at the Pointe and couldn't tell if it was those girls?" Todd was getting impatient.

"All we saw was the car, sir."

"Well," Jane said in a huff as she stood. "I'm calling the police and telling them what we just saw on the TV. I'm sure they're already on the case, but better safe than sorry."

"Mom, just wait!" Mavis was thinking fast. "I'm worried about her threats, especially if it is her. Calling the cops could make things worse. I promise, tomorrow, after school, Matt and I will go to the station and talk to the detective. But please, let me. I don't want you or anyone else to die because of being involved. Please!"

Todd sighed. "You two go to your room or the den. Jane and I need to talk."

"But no call right now?" Mavis asked.

"No call, I promise."

So, the two of them disappeared into Mavis' room. After fifteen minutes, they were called back out to face the parents.

"Here's the deal," Jane began. "We'll do it your way. But if you don't follow through, we will take control of this situation, end of story."

"We promise, we'll go tomorrow," they both lied in unison.

Satisfied, Jane excused the kids again, and they went to Mavis' room to have a chat before Matt left for work at the packing house.

"We better do some fast thinking, Mav," he said simply. "Hopefully, she leaves another body. If that's the case, to the cop shop, we go. But if not, we're going to stall. Trust me, I have some ideas already. You get some sleep, and I'll leave food tonight when I get off. See you in the morning for school?"

She nodded, and they kissed, and then Matt left. Mavis spent the rest of the evening showering and preparing for the next day of school, but her mind was preoccupied with the following day and her parents' wishes. She trusted Matt, she really did.

But this might just be too much for anyone to handle.

CHAPTER 20

The next day, the school had pretty much gone back to normal since the deaths of Leslie McCann and Bobby Carl. The football team held a vigil during last period, which most all of the Westside students attended, and a group of girls who had been close to Leslie, along with her parents, held a type of "In Memoriam" to the girl at the same time in the auditorium. Most who attended that particular time of mourning were mostly Greenville's affluent, and Mr. McCann made a huge deal out of donating an atrocious amount of money to Westside in Leslie's honor. It was to be used to start The Leslie McCann High School Scholarship Fund for the Exceptional. Which would fund the education of the most motivated and intelligent, enabling them to integrate college courses into their Senior Year studies without cost to them. Thus guiding them to realize their potential and become "the best they can possibly be, just as Leslie always had." Everyone seemed to ignore the irony that the girl was murdered while getting it on at Harbin's Pointe, but who cared?

While Mavis, Matt, Kim, Shawn, and the rest of those who attended the memorials were busy paying tribute and mourning, Shanice Hall was sitting on her sofa snacking on the last piece of kidney she had hoarded from last night's meal. It was extraordinary and rich, just as most male organs were, and Shanice was enjoying herself thoroughly.

The kidney belonged to a twenty-two-year-old security guard who kept watch during the night hours over a local manufacturing company called Kettlesen's Distribution. Shanice had parked her car down a dirt road half a mile from the gated entrance, then got his attention by claiming that she had been attacked and needed help. The good-looking man had tried to rush to her aid, unlocking the gate immediately, but he soon found himself to be supper. He had worn a white plastic name tag with the name Keith Martin engraved in black letters; Shanice had saved the nametag as a souvenir.

But she hadn't been so sloppy this time, leaving him lying right where she finished with him. Candy had ruined her ability to exhibit such reckless abandon. No, she had dragged him by his feet (and surprisingly he had been very easy to drag, which she attributed to her newfound strength) and put him into the company's incinerator with one easy toss. She followed that up with a pile of crushed cardboard boxes and a few clear plastic bags of garbage that were ready for burning beside the huge furnace unit. By the time she left the company property, she was feeling quite sharp and smug. Let them find this one, she thought.

As she had driven home, she had taken into consideration the importance of hiding her kills, at least until she got to the good ones, the ones that were aimed at Mavis. To slip up now would stir up the knowledge that the Cannibal Killer (as Candy had been dubbed by the media) was still on the loose, and soon they would all realize Candy wasn't the real culprit. She was no more than a victim of all of this, Shanice believed, and now her little plan of revenge included get-backs for her dead zombie best friend, dumb as she was.

The kidney was now gone, and she was tired of reminiscing. It was time to shower and clean up the blood a bit; it wouldn't do for anyone to come across any incriminating evidence. Blaming her period with this amount of blood would be hard. She had even gotten some on the brown leather couch. She dabbed away at the spots until they looked like water damage, then headed for the shower, then to bed. Tomorrow was a big day, and she would need her rest.

Yes, tomorrow was the new beginning. She was going to find her next partner in crime, but this time it would be a boy, a male, a man. Someone with half a brain and a heart nearly as dark as hers. That way she could share her plan of revenge without fear of it being screwed up by distraction and dimness. Best of all, she could have a little bit of good fun with her new minion. As the hot water of the shower ran over her rotting flesh, she contemplated what having sex would feel like as a zombie. Yes, he would be good looking, smart, and murderous.

He would be perfect.

Later, as she lay in her bed watching the TV and dozing, Shanice picked up a short piece on the news about her parents' bodies being found. She was nearly asleep when it caught her attention, but as soon as she heard the story, she began to laugh so hard she thought she might vomit up what was left of the kidney in her stomach. Well, it was official; she was being held captive by people looking for ransom. What a riot!

As soon as the story ended and Shanice relaxed, she fell asleep, dreaming of the guy who would soon help her start her army…

The guy who would help set off the war of Greenville.

∞

Matt had just left Mavis' house to go to work. Her parents were sleeping soundly in the next room. She was lying in her bed, baseball bat beside her, thinking about the afternoon. It had gone perfectly.

After all of the mourning at Westside, she and Matt had driven around Toledo, had a bite to eat, and did a bit of window shopping to pass the time. After all, they promised they would go to the cops, but neither of them had any intention of doing so. They had to pass the time to make it look legit.

When they had gotten back to Mavis', they told her parents a spun yarn concerning the police. Yes, they had gone to the station, and yes, they had made a report and shared the information they had. Lying seemed to come easier and easier when it came to her parents. The kids told the Harveys that the police were aware of Shanice Hall's presence, they believed she was posing as her mother and living in the area, and they had an All-Points Bulletin out for the girl under the guise of nothing more than questioning. The reports they were given on the news were meant to make Shanice relax and think she was in the clear. Soon, they told Todd and Jane, she would rear her ugly head, and the cops would pounce. She would slip up soon, Greenville detectives believed.

Mavis' parents bought it, which explained their sound sleep. But Mavis wouldn't sleep that night; she knew it was all malarkey. The truth was, she didn't care. If anyone got to Shanice, it would be her, and no one was going to take that away from her.

The TV played with a low volume, and she barely paid attention, she was so deep into her thoughts. But then she caught the beginnings of a story about a security guard at Kettlemen's Parts and Distributing who had been reported missing just a short time ago by his wife. She had tried to call him on his lunch break and received no answer. After calling his boss, the police were sent for a welfare check. As of one hour ago, the young father of a year-old son had not been located. His name was Keith Martin, and the news showed a recent photo. If anyone saw Keith, they were to call police immediately.

Mavis closed her eyes and sighed. She knew the truth deep inside, even at two in the morning. No one would be seeing Keith Martin any time soon. Shanice Hall had, indeed, wised up.

CHAPTER 21

Shanice woke with a feeling of motivation and invigoration, as well as an insatiable hunger for a raw human. Jumping out of bed, she stumbled to the kitchen and dug a bowl with a part of a lung in it out of the fridge. With that, she pulled out a Mason jar of blood, took off the lid; it wouldn't be as good as freshly harvested, but it would certainly fill the void and quiet the beast inside of her.

She inhaled the food; not even tasting it, just wanting the feeling of power, strength, and life that came with it. Soon, she was more than awake and invigorated, then quickly took a shower, and got dressed. She donned a pair of snakeskin-patterned skinny jeans, a cropped tank top, and some wedge heels. A brush through the hair, a bit of eyeliner and base makeup, and some mascara and blush, and Shanice looked alive again. Time to hit the road to find her "Prince Harming," as she had come to call the unknown person fondly.

She didn't have far to go or long to look, as it turned out. Shanice no sooner stepped off the lift into the underground parking garage than a loud, metallic sound far from the other end of the garage stopped her and caused her to spin in its direction. She froze in place and stared at the source of the noise: a very hot young man of about 23 was bending over and picking up a tire iron he had dropped on the concrete floor, which had made the loud clanging noise. Shanice continued to look at his exquisite form and inhale his scent as he straightened up tall, tire iron in hand.

"Uh, hi!" he greeted nervously, hollering at her pleasantly across the span of the garage, his voice echoing all around. "Sorry about the din; I guess I'm not much good at being quiet while changing tires."

It was a stupid ice-breaker, but he had the deepest and most articulate voice she had ever heard. Wow, was he hot! His dark hair hung just past the collar of his mauve button-down, which was neatly tucked into a crisp new pair of jeans. He wore casual, but perfect, black loafers, and a black belt was added at his waist. Shanice was not only stunned by his appearance, she thought she might be in love.

Placing the tire iron gingerly onto the trunk of his car, which was sporty and black, he turned back to her and flashed a million-dollar smile. "So, are you the new tenant?"

Shanice subconsciously pushed the butterflies in her stomach all the way back to her spine and smiled back her very best as well. "Yes. I'm Aneta Hall… but my friends call me Shanice. And you are?"

He started to close the gap between them with his hand out as if to shake hers. "Gunnar," he replied as he reached her and grasped her small hand. "Gunnar Reed. Well, Aneta, it seems we have the entire building to ourselves for the foreseeable future. I have to admit, I hope the other two units remain unsold for a while. I love the peace and privacy."

"Me too." Shanice's hand was burning when she pulled it away from his, partly from the natural warmth of his body, but mostly because of the powerful attraction she felt toward him. "So, how long have you lived here?"

Gunnar got a thoughtful look in his blue eyes. "Let's see, my parents purchased the unit for me while the building was still being renovated. It was a gift for my eighteenth birthday, and I moved in the day after. I just turned twenty-two, so I have been living in the huge building on my own for the last four years. I was nervous to meet you since I've become something of a loner living here, but I will say that all of my apprehension is gone now that we've… met."

His eyes sparkled at her as he spoke, and it was right at that moment that she knew she had found her partner. She wasn't sure how she knew, but it was clear deep down in her gut that this was the right person. A chill of excitement ran up her spine.

"So, it looks like you could use a little help changing your tire," she said shyly. "I have a bit of experience in this area if you don't."

Gunnar chuckled and blushed. "No, no. I've got it all under control. The iron just slipped from my hand; pretty embarrassing, actually." He stared at her, smiling for a brief moment, then asked, "Hey, since we're neighbors, would you like to have lunch sometime? After all, we should get to know each other."

Holding his gaze, Shanice replied, "I have a better idea. How about if I make you dinner tonight, and we eat at my place... if you're free, that is. That would give us plenty of peace, good food, and our choice of music. So, are you free?"

Amusingly, Gunnar didn't hesitate. "Yes! Um, I mean, what time should I show up?"

"How about six?" she asked. "We'll have a couple of drinks before dinner, eat a bit early, and maybe we can even hit a club or two if you feel comfortable."

Gunnar's blush deepened. "I'll be there, Aneta... I mean, Shanice."

With that, he went back to mend his car, glancing over his shoulder to smile at her twice. Shanice went to her car, but only for show. Now she didn't need to go on her little search at all. The perfect man had literally fallen into her lap, and she hadn't even reached her vehicle. But for show, she decided to leave and use the time to shop for food to cook for dinner and a new outfit. It would also be good to get her hair done, along with a manicure and pedicure.

The art of seduction was a heavy, heavy burden, but seduce him she would, and she would make him her very own possession. He would fall in love with her, live life with her as a zombie, and be the perfect companion in her new life.

But above all else, he would be her personal killing

machine.

But the problem was Mavis and Matt had no idea that Shanice had chosen another lackey, another person to transform from human to monster, one who she intended to help her bring Mavis down first.

Had they known, they would have realized that the real question was simply who would get to whom first, and Shanice had a lot more victims to choose from than Mavis did.

R.W.K. Clark

CHAPTER 22

For Shanice Hall, things were going beautifully.

Gunnar Reed had shown up for their dinner date looking like a sheer work of art. For dinner, she had prepared a wonderful combination of boring people food: T-bones cooked to perfection, baked potatoes with the works, asparagus with cream sauce, and for dessert, strawberry cheesecake. If she were honest, she prepared none of it herself; she had ordered it from a catering service and picked it up right before he arrived.

She also managed to dress in the most seductive fashion possible, basically using her appearance to tell him that he was getting lucky for sure. While Gunnar stuffed his face with the bland cooked food, Shanice picked at her own plate and listened to him talk on and on about his job, his parents, and his boring life, acting like he was the most interesting man she had ever met. She batted her eyelashes in all the right places and shot him flirtatious smiles that were highly effective in drawing him in. Before he even knew what hit him, they were making out on the couch, and in no time at all, she had delivered the fateful bite of the evening, a hard latch onto his upper arm that bled profusely. He hollered and screamed at her, dabbing at the wound with a paper towel while she smiled and let him rant.

Eventually, she had been able to calm him down, convincing him that she simply lost control in the heat of the moment. She sat him down and kissed his face and stroked his hair, thankful that she had eaten a pile of intestines before he came, otherwise she wouldn't have been able to stop herself from consuming him in full. By ten that night, he became excessively drowsy and fell asleep on the sofa. Shanice knew that this was the first sign that the change was taking place. Clearly, she remembered the same happening to her during her first night in juvenile detention after Mavis bit her; she had become so tired that she had fallen asleep at a table in the rec room while the group of hoodlums housed there watched TV. She had been helped to her cell by guards.

So, everything went as planned that evening, and in the morning she woke to find Gunnar sitting on her sofa, pale and feeling ill. It was easy to convince him to stay so she could "care for him," telling him he likely came down with a little bug. Taking the keys to his apartment, Shanice fetched some sweatpants, a t-shirt, and some socks and underwear for him to change into, then she tucked him into her own bed to sleep for the rest of the day, which Gunnar did easily. When she went out that night and dined on a young homeless man and dumped his carcass in the river, Gunnar didn't even miss her. As a matter of fact, he slept through the entire night.

But by morning, things were coming around full circle. When he woke, he was ravenous. She offered to make him steak and eggs, which he accepted, but instead of allowing her to cook for him, he tore through the raw steak and turned his nose up at the idea of eggs. He also devoured baggies full of liver, which she had split and saved from her homeless-man meal. Shanice watched him, pleased and eager to share what was happening with him as soon as he asked, which was right after he ate.

"What's wrong with me?" he questioned. "It seems like nothing sounds good if it's not bloody and raw. As gross as that sounds, it's delicious!"

Sitting him down on the sofa, she proceeded to fill him in, prepared for the worst of reactions. But to her great pleasure, he got excited. It seemed that he was enthralled with the idea of being "undead," and the thought of killing and dining on innocent people night after night put a sparkle in his eye that confirmed she had made the right choice.

But this time she also did something she hadn't done with Candy. Shanice explained fiercely that he should learn to control his urges, which he would do by listening to her at all times and following her every lead. Gunnar was so entranced by both Shanice and his new "life" that he eagerly agreed to everything, and she told him that his first test would be that very night.

The pair headed out as soon as darkness fell, driving into Toledo in his car, on which Shanice had replaced the license plate, after having stolen one off a similar black car while he slept. She had decided to take him into the city for his first kill because of the likelihood he may screw up in an overzealous state. In Toledo, there were more parks, more hidden options, and more chances of making a clean getaway. Also, she wasn't as concerned about getting rid of the body afterward, and she knew that it would be much easier to find a victim. Tonight, she intended to lure someone into the vehicle with them. Even though she preferred to eat men for a variety of reasons, she assumed he would prefer a female, and therefore she would target someone his age, using the hot guy with her to get the girl into the car and drive her to her demise.

Just as she hoped, everything went according to plan. It went so smoothly, in fact, that Shanice was amazed. Not only did Gunnar obey her every word, but he also did so with such gusto that she knew he belonged to her fully. On two separate occasions, she made him stop eating right in the middle of his feast, demanding that he control himself and do as she told him. Both times he complied immediately and easily. Shanice rewarded him as one would a dog, with words of approval and encouragement, even patting him on the head and stroking his hair as he went back to his meal.

They had taken the victim to a hiking trail in the woods, and then Gunnar bombarded her when Shanice gave him the signal. From there, Shanice found her own supper, ate and made sure to save the brain and a few organs for both of them so they could have a decent breakfast.

Shanice filled a cooler with the girl's remains leaving practically nothing but bones. When it was over, they simply left the girl lying in the dirt under debris just off the beaten path like a pile of trash. When they arrived back at her apartment, Gunnar showered and immediately passed out. He was exhausted from all the excitement, and from the rapid pace of his change. While Shanice cleaned up she thought about him and the way things had gone thus far; it was perfect. If things went this well for another week, she would take the next step in her plan of attack on Mavis, a step that would hit her enemy right where she lived.

An attack on her best friend, Kim Coleman.

CHAPTER 23

Mavis and her friends were all busy attending classes, studying, and trying to perfect their plans for Shanice. They were unaware that she had acquired another assistant, one who was much more obedient and adept than Candy Wilkes. As they lived their day-to-day lives and waited on pins and needles, Shanice was turning Gunnar Reed into a slave of the finest kind.

All during the next week, the kids were waiting anxiously, watching the news for word of missing persons or half-eaten bodies that had been found, but for some reason, nothing much seemed to be going on.

Mavis thought that maybe her enemy was having second thoughts, or better yet, had simply become so preoccupied with satisfying her own morbid appetite that she simply decided to put off her plans for Mavis' demise for a while. Perhaps the news about her parents caused her to go into hiding. Or maybe she even figured that it just wasn't worth risking being captured and put in prison or studied, or worse yet; put out of her misery for good.

By Friday morning, both Mavis and Matt were really beginning to wonder why Shanice had cut back on her food intake so much. They also began to get a little more lax in their caution, which was the worst mistake they could have made. Kim and Shawn were less wary as well with each passing day. Unbeknownst to all of them, their lack of vigilance was going to prove more detrimental than they could imagine.

Because even though there was no obvious sign of Mavis' arch enemy, she was not only still out there, she was going stronger than ever...

∞

Kim Coleman and Shawn Maher sat in his truck in the alleyway running behind Kim's house. They were shrouded in darkness, which was just the way they liked it after a Friday night date. It gave them the privacy they desired, which allowed them the freedom to kiss and make out to their hearts' content without Kim's mother or father looking out the front window of the house every five minutes. It was something of a ritual for them to sit in that alley and enjoy each other's company, which had very little to do with chitter-chatter.

Kim moaned as she pulled away from Shawn and looked up at him, both of their faces only slightly illuminated by the dashboard lights. "I can't wait until graduation when we are married. Then there will be no more alleys, no more nosy parents, none of that. Only you and me. Won't it be amazing?"

Shawn gave her another lingering kiss, then smiled. "I think about it all the time. It seems like the day will never come."

With a sigh, Kim glanced at the screen of her cell

phone for the time. "It's almost eleven; my parents are probably going nuts by now."

"They know we're out here," Shawn replied in a low tone as he tried to kiss her neck. "After all, we've been coming back here after our dates for months. Remember in June when your dad was taking out the trash and found us? I thought he was going to take off my head." Shawn tried to pull her back to him, but Kim firmly pushed him away.

"Babe, I have to get inside." She began to fluff her hair with her hands, trying to eliminate any signs of hanky-panky. "With all the crap going on they will worry themselves to death, and so will your mom and dad if you don't get home." She pulled a small compact from her purse and tried to get a look at herself in the dark without using the dome light. "Shanice sure has been quiet, though, don't you think? Wouldn't it be great if she just went back to wherever she came from?"

With a groan, Shawn adjusted himself in his seat. "I think she probably has, and none of us have anything to worry about. I mean, think about it, Kim. It's weird enough that Mavis has this little zombie problem. Don't you find it hard to believe that someone else does too?"

Kim shut the compact with a snap and gave him a stern look. "It sounds to me like you don't believe any of this to be true. That's really stupid, Shawn. After all, you saw Mavis eating the squirrel, and you know what Matt goes through to keep her safe and fed. Mavis is one of the best people I know; she wouldn't lie, and she doesn't want to hurt anyone. Why do you act like she is making all this up? What about all the missing people and dead bodies?"

Shawn offered up a shrug. "I don't know, Kim. I believe Mavis… I really do. It's just that, here she is, her and Matt, warning us about Shanice Hall, whom no one has seen since last school year. All of a sudden there are no more bodies, and to me, it all suddenly seems like some kind of scary movie that isn't real and never was." He turned to her and gave her a half-smile. "Know what I mean?"

Kim thought about it for a brief moment while she held his gaze, then she smiled back. "Yeah, I know what you mean."

Leaning forward, Shawn kissed her again, this time for a long and leisurely moment, before pulling away only slightly and touching the tip of his nose to hers. "I love you, you know. So, if we don't want to be reprimanded by your dad, you'd better go." Kim smiled and opened the door to the truck before turning to look at him one last time. "Kim? Just in case Mavis is right… I mean, all the way right, be careful on your way into the house."

"I will."

She hopped out and slammed the truck door behind her, then offered Shawn a wave and a smile. He started the truck and pulled up the alley, slowly at first, then drove to the street, took a right, and disappeared from her sight. Kim stood there for a second, then turned around and started for her house.

They had been parked almost at the alley's end, and

her house was in the middle of the block. There was only a single streetlight in the gravel-covered strip, located about ten feet from the gate in her fence. She gave the light a look, then shifted her eyes to the wooden garbage can rack that identified her own home. With a smile, Kim started to hum and took off walking slowly.

"Snap!"

She froze, stopping immediately, and began to look up and down the alley, squinting in the darkness. It seemed there were nothing and no one who made the sound. Raccoon, she thought, a chill running up her spine. Darn things were always finding their way into people's trash bins.

Kim started to walk once again, slowly and lightly, so as to not make as much noise on the gravel as she went. Suddenly, from almost directly behind her, a crash rang out loudly; it was the sound of a metal garbage can hitting the ground. She spun around and saw the can, only ten feet away, rolling back and forth gently on the ground. There was no raccoon, or human, to be seen. Her heart began to pound hard in her chest, and with her right hand, she reached into her purse for anything she could use to protect herself. The first thing she felt was an ink pen, her favorite, which happened to have a click mechanism. Kim wrapped her hand firmly around the pen and stared into the darkness as she pulled it out of her purse.

"Who's there?"

Her voice was in no way as loud or intimidating as

she would have liked it to be. As a matter of fact, it was shaking and almost sounded like a squeak. Her trembling hand gripped the ink pen and clicked the ballpoint open. It wouldn't smash a zombie's brain in, but it would certainly take out one of their eyes, or put a pretty good hole in their neck.

Another garbage can flew out and landed hard next to the first, crashing slightly into it before rolling a short distance away. Kim knew then that there was no raccoon in the alley; there was someone, but she also knew that the raccoon theory was now null and void.

"Shawn, if you're trying to scare me, you should know you're just pissing me off, so cut it out!"

Suddenly, a male form stepped out of the shadows. He took three steps toward her and stopped just to stare. Saying nothing, he stood there and looked at her, and in the small bit of light the streetlamp gave off, she could see he was smiling.

"Wh-who are you?" she stuttered.

He didn't respond. Instead, the man simply crossed his arms over his chest and continued to stare. Kim took a step backward, then another. That was when a second person stepped out of the shadows and stood beside him. This person began to chuckle, a deep, throaty sound that made Kim's stomach turn.

"Long time, no see, Kim."

It was Shanice Hall, and Kim knew it as surely as she knew her own name. Panic began to rise up in her throat right away, and she took another step back without even realizing she was doing it. Thoughts raced through her mind at break-neck speed: Mavis was right. Why did I get out of the truck? Where can I run to? If I take off now can they catch me? She really wouldn't eat me, would she?

But she knew the answer to every single question she asked herself. "What do you want, Shanice? I haven't done anything to you."

Shanice laughed. "I don't want anything. As far as what you have or haven't done, I'd say being friends with Mavis is enough. Don't you think she'll get the point a little more clearly if her best friend is part of the point?"

Kim took another few steps back, but this time, instead of standing there, watching in silence, the man took steps toward her. Just like Kim, he took three and stopped. Right at that second, she could have sworn her heart stopped completely.

Making sure she had an iron grip on that pen, Kim gave a nervous laugh and prepared herself to bolt. "So, uh, I suppose you think you're gonna be having me for your supper, huh, Shanice?"

Shanice gave a dazzling smile and waved her hand at Kim as though she was a bit silly. "Well, of course not! You know, I just can't really stomach the taste of the female of the species. But now, Gunnar here seems to really take to it. It seems to be his favorite... flavor."

With that, the man charged her, hitting Kim like a bull and knocking her back several feet. She didn't cry out, and she didn't put up a struggle. Instead, for the first time in her life her mind took over, and Kim

Coleman drew back with the ballpoint pen, closed her eyes, and buried its tip into whatever part of his body it came into contact with. Immediately, the man let out a guttural roar that almost deafened her. He jumped off of her, and all she could hear was the sound of pounding footsteps echoing through her ears and her brain.

Then Kim Coleman began to scream.

CHAPTER 24

"Now Kim, I don't care if it was only a small dog chasing you," Mrs. Coleman was scolding sternly. "We all know much more dangerous things are going on in Greenville right now, so stay out of the alley. And you are to go no place but home and school until further notice!"

Kim's mother walked out of the bedroom and closed the door a little harder than any of the four kids expected, making all of them jump a bit. After a moment, all of them exchanged glances, then Shawn spoke up to break the silence. He had a guilty look on his face, and his voice was low and still.

"I had a feeling I shouldn't have let you out of the truck right there," he said. "Now you've been chased by this dog, and it's all my fault."

Kim rolled her eyes and groaned. "Shawn, weren't you listening to anything I said before my mom came in? There was no dog! Sometimes I could swear you are on another planet!"

A confused look came over the football player's face. "No dog?"

"Oh!"

Mavis sat down on the edge of Kim's bed and gave her leg a pat to calm her down. "Just relax; he's just shaken up a bit."

"A big bit," Kim retorted sarcastically.

Now Mavis turned to Shawn. "Shawn, it was Shanice and some guy. Remember, we can't talk about the zombie thing in front of any adults."

He thought about her words for only a brief second before a look of both comprehension and rage came over his face. "You mean you were attacked by that stuck up girl that's been killing everybody?"

Matt, Mavis, and Kim all nodded in unison.

"I'll kill her!" he growled. "Mavis, we have to do something about this! Now she's really starting to get personal… and I'm getting pissed!"

"Calm down man," Matt said soothingly. Turning to Kim, he continued. "Now, tell us what happened, all the details, and start at the beginning."

So, Kim began to tell the story from the top. After only ten minutes, she got to the part where the strange guy had charged at her. The look on her face was both frightened and angry with the recollection.

"Then he was on top of me," she was saying as she stared at the ceiling. "It seems like I wasn't putting up much of a fight, but I must have, from the look of all the bruises on my arms. Oh, and the blood on my hands."

"Where did that come from again?" Mavis asked. "It couldn't have been from punching and scratching; there's just too much."

Kim shook her head. "No, it was my pen."

All three of her friends spoke at once again. "Your pen?"

Now Kim pulled herself up into a sitting position on her bed. "Yes! My pen! I forgot! I had heard all the noise, and that was when I reached into my purse for something I could use to protect myself. All I could feel in there was my click pen; you know, Mav, the one with the furry pink grip! Anyway, I got it out when I heard the noise, and that was where the blood came from. When that guy was on me, I stabbed him!"

Matt sat down on a stool next to Kim's desk. "You stabbed him with your pen? Where did you stab him?"

"Well," she continued thoughtfully, "at first I wasn't sure… I was so scared I just closed my eyes and stabbed. That was when he jumped off of me… fast! When I opened my eyes and started to scream, the two of them were starting to run, but he was close enough to me that I could see the pen sticking out of his… of his… his eye!"

"You stabbed him in the eye?" Shawn sounded blown away.

Kim simply looked at him and nodded. "And the pen was sticking right out of it! It was gross, but it was enough to make them both run away. I just kept on screaming until Mrs. Hoffman came running out of her back gate and found me. By then, neither Shanice nor the guy was around. They had gotten out of there fast."

Mavis turned and looked at Matt. "I wonder who this guy is."

"You read my mind," he replied. "It sounds to me like Shanice has managed to find herself another little helper."

There was a knock at Kim's bedroom door, then Mrs. Coleman opened it and stuck her head in. "Look kids. I know you are all concerned about Kim, but I think she'll pull through. It's time to clear out so she can get some sleep, okay?"

Mavis glanced at the bedside clock and saw that it was nearly one in the morning. "She's right, Matt. Let's get going; we'll let Kim and Shawn say goodnight alone."

The two of them said their goodbyes, promising they would be by to check on Kim the following morning, then they left the Coleman house and got into Matt's car. Cautiously, the pair locked themselves in the car, looking all around them as they did so. After a moment, Matt started the car, and they took off.

"It seems we're going to have to step things up a bit," Mavis said. "Shanice sure is, and from the way it sounds, she's got another minion helping her out."

Matt shook his head and made a noise of disgust. "I wonder who he is."

"Well, Kim says he looks older than us, so I doubt he's a student at Westside." Mavis' mind was racing, trying to recall any boyfriends that Shanice had during their years together in school. She could think of none that matched the description Kim gave of the stranger. "For all we know, he could be some poor, unsuspecting guy off the street."

"More than likely, that's exactly who he is," Matt said. After a moment, he continued. "Now what are we going to do, Mav? If we don't make a move soon, she is going to end up winning this little war."

He pulled the car into the Harvey driveway and shut off the ignition. The two of them sat there for a moment, just thinking and trying to figure things out in the silence. Mavis had a difficult time stringing two thoughts together, she was so sick over Kim's attack.

Suddenly, her cell phone rang. "It's probably my parents, worrying that I'm not home yet." She pulled the phone out of her back pocket and looked at the screen, then at Matt, her eyes wide. "It's Shanice, Matt!"

"Well, answer it!" he whispered harshly.

Mavis quickly swiped the screen and put the phone to her ear. "Hello?"

"Well, hello!" Shanice sounded cheerful but in a very evil way. "How did you like my little gift? I'll admit, it wasn't really finished, but I knew deep inside that you'd appreciate the thought behind it."

"Where are you, Shanice?" Mavis could feel the rage boiling up inside of her. "And who is your new friend?"

Shanice laughed long and hard. "Wouldn't you like to know. I have to say, little Kim surprised me with the ink pen to the eye routine. Gunnar won't be the same, but he really doesn't care. He was angry he didn't get to eat on time, but I made it up to him."

"Why are you doing this?"

In a mocking voice, Shanice echoed her words. "Why are you doing this? Why are you doing this? I'll tell you why I'm doing this: I despise you! I despise the fact that you get to live freely, and I have to sneak around and lie just to satisfy the appetite that you gave me."

"It hasn't been easy for me either," Mavis said. "But I make choices that won't hurt others, while you seem to get off on killing and harming. That's your problem, and no one else's."

She laughed again, but this time her laughter was much more sinister and controlled. "No, it is definitely your problem. Things are coming to a head. It would be simpler for you to just face me willingly. Otherwise, I am going to continue to do things this way. You will never know when or where to expect me. Is that really how you want it?"

Mavis glanced at Matt, who could obviously hear Shanice's words; he looked pissed. "What do you want me to do? What is it you want?"

"Simple," the girl replied. "I want you to be miserable for the rest of what we call life. I want you locked up somewhere, a guinea pig or research subject. I want you to be alone, the way I am alone. Think about it: if you want to save your friends and family you need to face me, and that's that. Let me know when you come to your senses."

With that, the call ended.

Mavis looked down at the screen, frustrated and angry. "We have to step things up, Matt."

"I heard," he replied.

Looking at him with a sad look, she said,

"Tomorrow the four of us need to meet and come up with something solid, and then we need to act. I'm not going to give her the satisfaction of giving her what she wants. I'll face her, but we will all do it together...

"And may the best zombie win."

CHAPTER 25

The following day was one of somber planning and piqued vigilance on the part of Mavis, Matt, and their two friends. Mavis and Matt knew that all four of them were the targets, even more so than their family members, but they wanted to deal with the issue at hand without really letting Kim and Shawn play a part.

Kim wanted to be right in the middle, however. The first thing that morning, Mavis got a phone call from an angry and vengeful Kim, who was full of bright ideas and boundless courage when it came to finding and stopping Shanice. But Mavis wanted to keep her best friend as far out of the equation as possible. To appease Kim, she listened to what she had to say, agreed in all the right places, and then distracted the girl with other topics.

Kim wanted to go directly to Shanice's loft and simply take her out. It took quite a bit of convincing to get the girl to understand that the repercussions of such a plan would be terribly detrimental. Mavis promised to take the idea to Matt and fine-tune it, but she knew that they wouldn't be taking that course of action at all. As a matter of fact, she knew that when the final confrontation did happen, Kim wouldn't be there, and neither would Shawn, not if she could help it.

Ten minutes after she hung up with Kim, she ate some leftover cow tongue that Matt had brought her the day before and that she had kept in her trusty cooler. It wasn't fresh, but it took the edge off so she could think. Mavis was no sooner finished cleaning up from her meal than Matt showed up.

"I think it's time for us to get down to business," he said as soon as her bedroom door was closed and locked. "Where are your parents?"

"They are at Grandma Cabot's for the day," she replied. "It's the time of year that Grandma starts getting her garden ready for the fall and winter, so they'll have their hands full. They made me promise not to leave the house at all unless I'm with you, and I can't leave at all after dark, even in your company. So, we need to use our time wisely."

Matt plopped down in the chair at her desk. "Okay, so first things first. This morning I went and stalked out Shanice's place in my mom's minivan. She had the one-eyed guy with her, and I overheard her calling him 'Gunnar.' I did a bit of research on the computer, which turned out to be easy, considering the oddness of his name. There is only one Gunnar in all of Toledo and the surrounding area: Gunnar Reed, twenty-two, with the same address as Shanice's; he just owns a different unit. Looks like she basically 'zombie-fied' her neighbor. He's wearing a patch and following her around like a puppy dog, so I'm positive we can bet that Gunnar

Reed is the one who attacked Kim in the alley."

"While Shanice watched and egged him on."

Matt nodded. "Exactly."

"Well," Mavis continued, "I just got off the phone with Kim, and she is determined on being right in the middle of this. I don't want her or Shawn in the mix at all. I think we should handle it… or I should alone, whatever makes you feel the most comfortable. Matt, this is coming to a head fast. If you don't want to be involved, I don't blame you. After all, they can't kill me. I just want all of you safe."

Matt shot a slight glare in her direction. "Mavis, I wouldn't back out now for a million dollars. Shanice has gone too far with all of this. We'll handle this together, understand? So, no more offering to let me step down or anything like that. I'm in it for the long haul, so no more crap."

Mavis gave the nod and dropped the subject. "Okay, Gunnar Reed is her slave. So, we have you and me against the two of them; at least the numbers are equal. What do you want to do?"

Matt gave a slight smile. "Well, while it's not perfect, this is my plan so far…"

He proceeded to tell her that he wanted to meet them the following Saturday night at eleven. They would meet at Donnelly Park, on the edge of the woods near the disc golf course's starting point. Together, they would take care of the two zombies, fighting them basically "to the death."

"But you seem to be forgetting one thing," Mavis

said. "You are human; you can be killed, and it will be permanent. There is no way they are going to let you live by simply biting you; they're going to take you out but good."

Matt nodded. "I understand your concerns; I have the same ones. But I also have a couple of helpful resources that will make me a bit safer. First, my father used to train police dogs in Cleveland before he joined his firm. Anyway, he has a couple of those thick protective suits they use during training. They're hard to move around in, but I've worn and played in them several times in my life, and I'm pretty good. I'll be wearing one of those... full gear."

Mavis smiled and nodded. "Nice, I like it. What else?"

"I also have a fish bat that I'm going to customize."

Mavis was immediately confused. "A 'fish bat'?"

He nodded. "A fish bat is used to hit fish over the head after you catch them when fishing. It puts them out of their misery with only a blow or two, and it's small, so it's easy to get a good thump on. So, I'm going to drill out my fish bat about halfway and fill it with concrete. I'll fit it with a strong leather strap, so it hangs from my wrist and gives me good momentum when swung. The first thing I'm going to do is cave in Gunnar Reed's head; that will cut things in half for little Shanice."

Mavis liked it. "That will allow me to deal with Shanice face-to-face, which is exactly how she wants it. And to be honest, it's how I want it, too. Especially at this point in the game. So, we just don't tell Kim or Shawn. I will call Shanice and set it up, and then we keep quiet. What if she wants the others there?"

Matt shrugged. "Easy. We just tell her they will be; we lie."

"Good enough." She thought for a minute. "That gives us an entire week of downtime. Shanice and her puppy dog will be killing all week, Matt. What do we do about that?"

Leaning forward, Matt looked Mavis square in the eye. "There is nothing we can do about it but let it happen. It's sad, and it leaves us feeling pretty horrible, I know, but this is how it is."

There was nothing more to think about or argue. "You're right. Okay, so we just go to school and make sure our families are safe and sound in the meantime. Well, I'm going to try to stipulate that if she wants to meet me no killing can be done."

Matt shook his head. "No. Just let things go the way they're going to go. Come Saturday, if she agrees to meet us, we'll put a stop to it. But for now, she isn't going to take any demands, and you know it, Mav. Now, call her."

She glanced down at the phone sitting next to her on the bed, then took a deep breath and picked it up. Mavis quickly dialed Shanice's number and put the cell on the speaker; it rang only twice before the girl picked it up. From the tone of her voice, Mavis could tell she was pleased to hear from her.

"Well, well, well," she greeted. "I thought I may be

speaking to you soon, but I didn't think it would be today. How can I help you, Mavis Harvey? Have you finally come to your senses and decided to stop the madness by handing yourself over to me?"

Mavis closed her eyes and shook her head in disgust. "That isn't what I had in mind at all. But I do think we need to face each other and take care of things once and for all."

"What did you have in mind?"

"Donnelly Park," Mavis replied. "One week from today at eleven at night. It will be myself and Matt Morgan, my boyfriend, against you and Gunnar, your new lackey. No one else, just the four of us."

Shanice was silent for a bit. "How did you know Gunnar's name?"

"That's beside the point, Shanice." Mavis could tell that the girl was now on the defense, if only slightly. "He's one of us now, so I'm okay with him joining in the fun and games."

"But Matt Morgan isn't," was Shanice's retort. "Are you seriously willing to put him at such risk?"

Mavis looked at Matt, a sick feeling in her stomach. "Is any of that really your business?" she asked. "Does it pertain to you, or our little battle, in any way? You would think you'd like the idea of someone weaker being so exposed to your horrors."

Shanice laughed. "I'll admit that I look forward to sinking my teeth into him."

"That won't be happening." Mavis took a deep breath. "I also wish you could be trusted to find other means of nourishment this week that don't involve murder."

Another laugh. "Don't kid yourself, Skippy. Oh, what about Kim and her big lug? I expected them to be there as well. What will my sweet Gunnar eat? He prefers girls, and you aren't edible."

"Shanice, they will not be there," Mavis spoke the words with firm harshness. "While I can't expect you to agree to not killing this week, I do expect you to leave my friends and family alone... and I mean alone. Do you understand? If you do not comply, we will not only not meet on Saturday, but I will go to the police and hand you over to them on a platter, along with myself."

"You wouldn't."

Mavis was smiling now. "I absolutely will. So, Saturday night, just the four of us. And be on time; got it?"

"I'll see you then," Shanice replied smoothly. "And don't get all nervous and go to the cops. I'll follow the rules. Or should I say, that one rule? No family, no friends."

This time, Mavis hung up first. "It's done."

Matt sat back in the chair and nodded. "Saturday night it is."

∞

It was still the weekend, so they decided that, when Matt got off work on Sunday night, the two of them would sneak away and spy on the loft building. They would try to see what Shanice was up to in her spare time if she had any kind of particular routine whatsoever. They would have to formulate a more perfect plan from there.

CHAPTER 26

While Mavis was fretting, and Matt was reassuring, and Kim was coming unglued, Shanice Hall was having the time of her life.

Right after getting the call from Mavis to set up the Donnelly Park meeting, Shanice took Gunnar, and the two of them went on something of a celebratory free-for-all. They went on a controlled killing spree for their nourishment, and they showed no care or concern for getting caught at all. It didn't matter who their victims were or how their bodies were left, Shanice and Gunnar attacked, ate, and let the spoils lie. The actions of the next six days served a couple of purposes. First, it fed them, yes, and they kept some for breakfast. But the second purpose was a bit more sinister; they left the bodies for sheer entertainment. Watching the public panic and Mavis scramble around, plotting and scheming, which made Shanice laugh. Sure, to Gunnar it was all about food; but to Shanice, their actions were something of a signature, an autograph which she was signing for her biggest fan, Mavis.

Shanice had more fun that week than she had since all of this began. Once she knew for sure that Mavis was going to meet her and Gunnar for the showdown, she stopped caring about slowing down the process of getting caught. When Mavis made the comment about turning herself in just to bring Shanice down, she knew for sure she was safe. Mavis didn't want to get caught any more than she did. She wanted to meet and fight this thing out like she should, and that fact made Shanice want to party like a rock star. That was why she left bodies strewn everywhere. It was her way of telling Mavis she could take a leap off a cliff.

Mavis was busy wading her way through the tension, worry, and the safety of her loved ones. Shanice basically had herself a good old time with her new friend and confidante, Gunnar Reed, but she didn't waste all of her time just messing around. She decided that Gunnar also needed to have a bit of "training" if he was going to go up against Mavis. Since Mavis was going to be his combat "pal," as Shanice called it, she would put him through a bit of schooling to make sure that he at least put up a good fight. She would be focusing on Matt, of course, because Matt would be her meal, and Gunnar would be the distraction. Shanice wasn't worried about Matt; he would be wiped out in the first ten minutes of the fight, especially since he was to be facing her, in all of her zombie glory. The thought made her smile, then laugh out loud.

But Gunnar would be going up against Mavis, distraction or not, and Mavis had been in her current condition for far longer than he. Of course, regardless of her Gothic look and strange ways, Mavis didn't have a mean bone in her body. When it came to those she cared about, Shanice didn't have a single doubt that the girl's lack of experience fighting would have no bearing on the outcome; she would likely mop up the floor with Gunnar. For one thing, he would be thinking food, and Mavis wasn't fit for him to eat. He was still too much of a "baby," so to speak. Sure, he made Candy look like a moron in this state, but he still didn't have a firm grasp on what he had become or who he now was. Mavis would be the victor; there was absolutely no doubt about it.

∞

The week went on in this way, for both Mavis, and for Shanice. While Mavis obsessed over the safety of those she cared about, Shanice obsessed over their demise. The result of this was that Mavis was getting stronger and more determined, while Shanice only became more obsessed and prideful.

Every single day that passed increased this process more and more. The funny thing was that Shanice was willing to bet on her victory, while Mavis maintained a level of humble doubt. What if Matt was killed? What if she was taken into custody and studied like a newfound species of insect? How would that affect her parents, Todd and Jane? It would ruin their lives, as well as the lives of Mr. and Mrs. Morgan.

But all Shanice could think about, in her selfish, self-indulgent state of mind, was how it would affect her if she lost. Her mind had her convinced that she would win, hands-down, but something inside of her was tugging at her as if trying to tell her that she needed to prepare for any outcome. Every time she felt that tug, she simply ignored it and pushed it down as far to the base of her being as she could, until it dulled and was forgotten.

∞

Matt and Mavis discussed the details of all of this each and every day, though they didn't bring up any of it to either Shawn or Kim. Shawn was easy to dodge, he wasn't the brightest person in their little group. Once a couple of days had passed after Kim's attack, he let his anger, and his fear, fade. But Kim was still a bit wound up, and she was eager to confront Shanice, so she made it a point to contact Mavis each day to ask if a meeting had been set up. Every time Mavis lied to her friend, denying any contact with the girl, and telling Kim that no meeting had been arranged. She didn't feel bad about the lies; Mavis felt like telling them was for the best interest of her friend.

With two new bodies being found every day, she was literally on the verge of hysteria, controlling it only with her anger at the situation. It was all Mavis could do to reason with her during their first real telephone discussion on the matter.

"Mavis, I know you're not going to just let this drop," Kim was saying. It was very early in the morning, before school or even breakfast. "The very fact that Shanice is continuing to kill, and is leaving bodies lying around like empty soda cans, is enough for me to know you have something up your sleeve."

Mavis hated lying to her best friend. In the past, before all of this started, she had confided every aspect of her life to the girl. She eventually shared the truth with Kim once Matt moved to Greenville and helped her understand what was happening. But this was different; she was telling an outright untruth, and she was doing it on purpose. It didn't matter to Mavis' heart that it was for Kim's own good. All that mattered was that she was doing it.

"Kim, I'm telling you that Matt and I have both tried to call," Mavis replied, adding enough enunciation to the words to make them sound convincing. "Not only that, we have sat outside her apartment on several occasions. If we see her, we plan to confront her then and there, especially if she doesn't talk to us."

Kim made a sound that expressed her doubt clearly, then followed with "Hmmm…" After another moment, Kim continued. "Listen, I know I'm not the smartest person in the world… or on my block, for that matter. But the last time we talked about all this together, on Friday after that guy attacked me, dealing with Shanice Hall was all we could talk about. Now, suddenly, she starts killing like an attack dog, we know it's her, and you're just like, 'Oh if we run into her, we'll deal with it.' I don't think I believe you, Mavis."

Those words hurt Mavis more than she ever would have guessed, but it was only because they were true. This was the way it had to be right now, for Kim, for Shawn, and for both of their families. If Mavis had her own way she wouldn't even involve Matt, but he wasn't about to duck out, or let her shove him into a corner. He wanted to keep her safe and free, and the only way Matt could be sure that got done was to be directly involved in this little zombie war. He would be; even if it cost him his own life.

"Kim, when I hear from her, or even if I see her, you will be the first person I tell," Mavis had reassured. "Now, just try to focus on school and studies; it will make the time go faster."

That had been on Wednesday. Kim had given Mavis an almost identical call on Thursday evening, only that time she was a bit more demanding and sharp. In school that day, she had seemed fine, even though Mavis and Matt saw her only on a couple of brief occasions. By the time Friday rolled around. However, Kim didn't even bother with the phone. She confronted Mavis during their lunch period and even raised her voice a little. During the ride home from school, Matt and Mavis discussed her behavior, which bordered on irrational.

"I just can't figure Kim out," Mavis was saying as Matt navigated the way home in his car. "You know, there was a time she would have believed every word I said, just because it was coming out of my mouth. Why is she so difficult?"

Matt took a right turn before he replied. "Think about it, Mav. For someone taking psych classes, you sure seem to be a little thick in the head about this. She was violently attacked last Friday, remember? And the attack was done by zombies that she has been warned about. It was only by luck that she is still walking the planet… saved by a click pen, anyway. If you were her, wouldn't you want to get something done? Wouldn't you be afraid?"

After a moment of thought, Mavis said, "Of course, but it's for her safety. I would never lie to her just to lie, Matthew."

"I know, but maybe she thinks you're doing nothing at all. Did you ever think of that?"

Matt dropped her off at home right after that, promising that he would bring her breakfast in the morning. Even he didn't feel safe getting dropped off after eleven. His parents would be taking him and picking him up anyway, he had to get his car home so his mom could drive him. Mavis planted a kiss on his lips and thanked him for all he did before getting out.

"Well, tomorrow is the night," she said as she searched his face with her eyes. "Are you sure… you're okay with this? I mean, I can deal with it, Matt."

He immediately shook his head. "Maybe if it were just you and Shanice, but she has this Gunnar character, and I just don't feel comfortable with the numbers or the odds. Listen, Mavis, I'm going to be fine. I've pretty much mastered my fish bat, and I'm moving around in that awkward bite suit like it's a second skin… well, not quite, but close. There is nothing you can do or say to get me to back out, got it?"

"Got it."

The two of them kissed once more, this time for a long time, and when they were done, they embraced for several seconds as well.

"I love you, Matt," Mavis whispered into his ear.

He whispered back, "I love you too, Mavis… more than you know."

Without looking him in the eye so he wouldn't see her fear and sadness, Mavis quickly jumped out of the car and ran up the walk to the front door of her house without looking back. She didn't want to look as weak and frightened as she felt; she didn't want him to see that she was scared stiff of what might happen the next night.

But for now, she would practice in her room to prepare. She would watch every zombie movie that night she could get her hands on. First, she would call Kim and make sure that her friend was okay, then she would eat supper with her family and follow it up with a pig kidney. After that, she would hit the DVDs and see if she could learn anything about how vicious zombies fought. She may not have a vicious bone in her body, but it was time for her to learn how to act like one.

Time was passing quickly… much too quickly for her taste.

∞

While Mavis was busy watching zombie movies like she was cramming for a zombie test, Shanice was having long talks with Gunnar, drilling into him the facts about Mavis and himself, and expressing the importance of focus and judgment. He asked many questions about the end result; such as could he eat her once they had won? Of course not, she told him over and over; Mavis was a zombie-like they were, and it would be like eating rotten food for him.

By Friday morning, Shanice was confident that she had Gunnar sufficiently prepared, and she knew that she was, but she felt she needed a backup plan of some kind. Why? She wasn't sure. Yes, she was confident in her success on Saturday, but something inside was telling her that she needed to have some kind of insurance, just in case.

So, she began to let her wheels turn. While Gunnar rested that morning, she began to think about what would effectively give her the upper hand when it came to the pending battle. Simple threats weren't going to work; neither would bringing adult family members into the situation. That choice would succeed in doing nothing but getting her caught for sure. If there was one thing she knew with confidence, it was that getting caught would only get her, and her alone, into trouble. Zombie or not, Mavis was somehow functioning and fully responsible. She had chosen to follow the light inside of her instead of the darkness, and she was succeeding. Shanice had chosen to jump head first into the abyss of blackness inside of her as soon as it offered itself to her. Why? She knew the answer; she didn't have to ask. She was black inside way before Mavis ever bit her.

Then, like a bolt of lightning, the solution came to her. She knew exactly how to get the upper hand. Shanice knew precisely what she could do to gain control over the battle, and ultimately win the war. All she had to do was a little bit of stalking and research, and she would have it all figured out.

She grabbed her car keys and purse, left Gunnar a note telling him she would be back, and reminding him of the leftovers in the fridge for breakfast, then she headed out. Time to do a bunch of watching, listening, and learning. Shanice had very specific people in mind to serve as the "insurance," but she needed to know what they were going to be doing right before the meeting at the park.

She fully intended to discover every last detail.

CHAPTER 27

By Saturday morning, Mavis was beginning to feel more confident about the meet in the park. Matt seemed to have his eggs in one basket, and she had Kim and Shawn convinced that things were actually letting up. So, when the phone rang that morning, and the screen showed it to be Kim, Mavis wasn't nervous or full of dread at the possibility of her nagging at all. She answered cheerfully, even in the midst of her nervousness, so that Kim wouldn't get suspicious.

"Good morning," she greeted. "What's up with you today?"

Kim didn't miss a beat. "Not much; just another Saturday… at least, so far. How about you? Any plans?"

"Um, no. Probably hang out with Matt and get our homework done early," Mavis replied. "You know after he gets off work. He took the early shift today, so he'll be free to spend the evening with me for studies."

Kim was still for a bit, then she said, "I got a call from Shanice Hall a few minutes ago."

If Mavis' heart had been functioning, it would have skipped a beat. "Shanice? What the heck did she want with you?"

"Well," Kim said slowly, "she wanted to apologize. You know, for the incident in the alley and all."

Mavis mind started spinning. Shanice? Apologizing? What was really going on?

"What all did she say?" she asked.

Kim sounded apprehensive. "Before I go any further, I should apologize for doubting you. Shanice told me you wouldn't be meeting because she is starting to get over her anger. She said that the only reason she and her boyfriend had gone on the killing spree this week was because they were mad that I got away, but she is seeing a reason now. She also said she is considering changing her ways, that she now sees how she has been her entire life, and that she feels a bit guilty for her cruel behavior."

"Kim, nothing you are telling me sounds right," Mavis said cautiously. "I mean, come on, we have known Shanice our whole lives practically. Have you ever known her to care about anyone but herself? I mean, come on, a leopard can't change its spots."

Her friend took a deep breath. "I thought the same thing, but she sounded so sincere. She also told me she heard that Shawn and I were planning to, you know, get married after graduation. She said she thought we make a great couple, and she wishes the best for both of us. She also said that I don't have anything to worry about anymore. Neither she nor Gunnar will be putting you or your family and friends in danger anymore. As a matter of fact, they are going to be figuring out how to live the zombie life the right way. What do you think of all that?"

Mavis paused confusion set in her mind and heart like never before. "I think something isn't right, Kim," she said. "I mean, I can't exactly say why, but I think we should all still tread lightly. Even more so, as a matter of fact. Why would someone like Shanice suddenly change her ways?"

"I don't know, but she had a set of tickets to that new movie, *High School Honeys*, couriered over just after I got off the phone. She said it was her way of making up for the attack." Kim took a breath that Mavis could tell was all about being relieved. "It's for the seven o'clock showing. I'm excited; you know I've wanted to see that show. Now Shawn doesn't have to worry about getting tickets. Wasn't that a nice gesture?"

"Kim, I don't think the two of you should go to that show." Mavis wasn't sure why, but she was certain that Shanice had something horrible up her sleeve, and it involved Kim and Shawn.

Now Kim gave a frustrated grunt. "She told me I shouldn't tell you and that you would come up with some crazy reason why we shouldn't go. And she said that you wouldn't trust her change of heart. I guess Shanice was right on all counts. Well, Mavis, let me tell you something: not everything is about you, or about your being a zombie. Besides, maybe she really does feel bad. People do have changes of heart every day. Maybe Shanice really sees that it's going to get her nowhere to fight and battle with you and to hurt everyone she sees. I told her that if you can live as a zombie without killing everyone, so can she. She really was very nice; maybe you should give her a call yourself."

"Yeah, Kim, you're right," Mavis replied thoughtfully. "I think I will."

"Good," her friend said, then she immediately hung up.

Mavis stared at her cell phone for a long time. She was tempted to call Shanice Hall right then and there, and ask her what the heck she was up to. But she also knew it wouldn't do any good; the girl would just be syrupy sweet and every word out of her mouth would be a lie. All Mavis knew was that Shanice was up to nothing but no good and that if she didn't figure out what it was, more people were going to get hurt. She looked at the time: 10:30 in the morning. Matt wouldn't be off work until two, and he wouldn't get to her house until 2:30 after his dad took him home to pick up his own car. She decided it would be best if she waited on him before calling Shanice. He would be able to help her deduce what the girl was up to.

Tucking her phone into her back pocket, Mavis went out into the backyard to help her mother get some end-of-season yard work done and wait for Matt. She kept her calm façade intact but inside she was beside herself with worry. Shanice Hall was one of the most devious individuals she had ever known, and she was sure that her "kind" gesture toward Kim and Shawn was simply laced with some kind of poison that would lure them to a place they didn't want to be. Mavis felt sick to her stomach over the whole thing.

The worst part of it all was that she had only about twelve hours to figure it out; the clock was ticking faster than she liked, and there was nothing she could do to stop it.

CHAPTER 28

As always Matt showed up on time, with bells on and the mini cooler in his hand. That day he brought Mavis extra sustenance because of the impending battle that night. He wanted her to be on her toes. He also had a large garbage bag which held his dad's old bite suit and his customized fish bat. Matt was anxious to show everything to Mavis so she would feel better about the fight and his safety.

As soon as he arrived, the two of them went into her room. Instead of sitting right down to eat, Mavis tucked the cooler away under her desk for later. Matt started to unpack the bite suit, but Mavis stopped him right away. They had more important things to go over first.

"What's going on?" Matt asked, putting the garbage bag with the suit aside. "Don't you want to check it out?"

Mavis sat down on the bed and nodded. "Yeah, but we need to have a serious talk first."

Sitting down at the desk, Matt gave her a serious look. "What's going on? I know you're nervous about tonight, but it's going to be fine. You look like you're ready to back out. You have to forget about the new victims; this is about saving our future."

"This has nothing to do with backing out," Mavis said as she stood up and started to pace. "I talked to Kim a few hours ago; she got a call this morning from Shanice, and I have to tell you, the girl is seriously up to no good."

Matt's attitude changed immediately. "What is she up to now?"

It seemed that Shanice was much more conniving than they had been expecting, and both of them felt a sense of unease over it. Of course, she wasn't backing out of the meet. If she were, Mavis would have definitely heard from her by now. No, she had something slimy and slippery hidden up her sleeve. She was doing her best to somehow involve Kim and Shawn, even though Mavis had refused to bring them into the situation.

"You tried to talk her out of going, didn't you?" He was referring to Kim and the movie. "I mean, all you have to do with Kim is express to her clearly that Shanice has something really bad planned. She'll believe you… didn't you try?"

Mavis felt immediate frustration and shot Matt a look to kill. "Of course, I warned her not to go. As a matter of fact, I expressed to her that Shanice was up to terrible business somehow, but it seemed to me that Kim was almost… I don't know… slightly brainwashed somehow. She just wouldn't listen to me. Actually, she acted like I was hiding something from her like I hadn't been completely honest from the start. That was the impression I got, anyway. Heck, I don't know what to think or do."

Matt didn't answer her right away; he was deep in his own thoughts as he tried to sort out the mess in his mind. "Let's just start at the beginning," he muttered thoughtfully after a long moment. "We are just running in place... panicking. This isn't going to do anyone any good. Now, you told Shanice clearly that neither family nor Kim and Shawn were to be involved, right? At least, that's what I heard, and the phone was on speaker when you set the time for the meet."

"That's exactly right," Mavis replied. She was pacing furiously now, her mind completely convinced that Kim and Shawn were in trouble. "I told her that it would be her and Gunnar, against you and me. No alternatives, no compromise."

Matt stood now, and he began to pace behind her; the two of them would wear a circle in the floor if they weren't careful. "So, all of a sudden, Shanice decides to turn over a new leaf and just buy movie tickets for the two people who won't be attending the meet. They happen to be the two people she wanted there." He stopped suddenly and grabbed Mavis' arm, turning her to face him. "You don't think she's going to try to snatch them, do you? I mean, while we're waiting for her and Gunnar, they're across town eating them?"

Mavis stopped in her tracks. "Oh, I thought of a lot of things, but I didn't think of that. I need to call Shanice now!"

Without waiting for Matt to respond, Mavis grabbed

her cell and soon had a ring on Shanice's line. After two rings, she picked up. The girl sounded cheerful, almost to the point of being entertained.

"Hello?"

"Shanice, it's Mavis." Her tone was short and slightly angry. "I want to know what you have done as far as this movie ticket crap with Kim and Shawn Maher."

Her nemesis giggled slightly. "Whatever are you talking about, Mavis? I just thought they could use a stress-free evening after all I've put them through. Perhaps you and your man could as well; I hadn't thought of that."

"Cut the crap, Shanice!" Mavis was livid; she was even shaking violently in her anger. "Kim and Shawn are to have nothing to do with our face-off, and I swear, I will turn myself in for what I am if you try to involve them in any way!"

Shanice took a dramatic breath and began to cluck her tongue as if scolding a naughty child. "Mavis, right now you need to worry about the task at hand. If you want to turn yourself in, go for it, but your decision will have no effect on me whatsoever. Anyway, I told you that they are not required to come to the meet… so no worries."

Shanice sounded convincing, but Mavis knew that it was all garbage. Even if somehow Kim and her boyfriend ended up there, or if Shanice didn't show and she and her sidekick ate them, what good would it do to turn herself in? Mavis was between a rock and a hard place, and she knew it. No matter what route she went or what "rules" she made, Shanice would do whatever she wanted to do. Mavis simply had to move forward and hope for the best.

In a deathly still voice, Mavis growled, "Don't you dare hurt my friends. You need to just do the right thing, for once in your life, and go by the rules we set, Shanice. Leave Kim, Shawn, and everyone else out of it."

"Even Gunnar?" Shanice put on a false air of incredulity. "I have to tell you: I think you would really like Gunnar. Not only is he incredibly good looking, but he really knows how to take a bite out of a good conversation!" She burst into laughter, guffawing at a level that was pretty much out of control.

Mavis groaned helplessly, shook her head, and hung up the call. Turning to Matt, she said, "She's positively impossible. We just can't guarantee that she is going to do anything on the up and up. Matt, we are taking a huge risk by meeting her and this Gunnar guy. I think that we have a fairly good chance of coming out on the bottom of this dogpile… and I also think I'd have a better chance of coming out ahead, that all of us would if I just went to the police."

"Mavis, stop!"

Immediately, she stopped her fretting and turned her eyes to him, but they were wide and full of worry. The look on Matt's face betrayed his anger; he saw all that Shanice was doing as nothing more than tactics of manipulation meant to disrupt her confidence and keep her from facing Shanice. This fact, in turn, told him something else: Shanice was nervous about the meet herself. If she weren't, she wouldn't go to such lengths to frighten Mavis and put her on the defense.

"Mavis, I need you to sit down and listen to me," he said softly. "I think that you need to face some facts."

She stared at him for a brief second, then plopped down on her bed and waited for him to say what was on his mind.

"Now, listen. Shanice is bad, through and through, and we both know this," he began. "I believe that Kim knows it, too, even though Shawn may be a bit dense to the fact. Anyway, every time she does something… like this, for instance, all she is trying to do is get you shook up. That way, you will either duck out of the meet, or you will be such a mess when we do arrive. She will have rendered you helpless and weak… do you understand?"

Mavis thought about it for a second and then nodded. "Yes, I get it. But how is sending tickets to Kim and Shawn going to accomplish that?"

Matt held his hands out to her as if motioning in her direction. "Isn't it obvious? Look at you already? You're an emotional mess, filled with insecurity, and almost convinced that she is going to have them eaten before we arrive. What if she did this to keep them away so that we can have this battle out without Shawn or Kim running and calling the cops? Also, she could have other reasons that we don't understand, but remember, you are the main goal, not Kim, and not Shawn… got it?"

Mavis nodded, her mind tired and her emotions ready to cave in. Matt was right, no matter what kind of crap Shanice was up to, she had to maintain some kind of level head and strength. The time to meet the girl was nearly upon them, and she couldn't crumble now.

Matt looked at the clock on the nightstand. "Okay, Mavis, it's just after three. We have eight hours to be sure that our heads are on straight and that we are strong enough to Shanice and her puppet that we aren't going to tolerate the things she is pulling. So, if I were you, I would try to calm and rest my mind, then I would eat some of the food I brought you. We'll both have to eat supper with your parents, then we'll get ready to head to Donnelly once your parents are sleeping. So, set your mind, get yourself calm, and do the best you can to get your mind off Kim and Shawn, got it?"

Mavis squared off her shoulders and nodded at him with determination. "Got it. What are you going to do?"

"I'll tell you what: you take a nap, and I'll make sure I'm ready with this suit. I'll be quiet, so I don't disturb you."

She wasn't sure if she could sleep, but she was willing to try. Lying down on the bed, she watched Matt as he struggled his way into the bite suit. It didn't take her long to begin to doze off, and soon she was completely asleep. It was then that the dreams came on.

∞

Donnelly Park was darker than usual, and it was so quiet that it seemed she could hear every single animal that lived within its perimeter. The only light came from a pole lamp situated in the parking area. It gave off a dim version of illumination that was hardly enough to cast a shadow, but it was enough for Mavis to tell that she was in the lot nearest to the beginning of the golf course, which was exactly where they were to meet Shanice.

She looked down at her watch and saw that it was only three minutes to eleven. "Looks like she is going to be late, but I'm not surprised," Mavis said. "She was late for nearly every class in school, so why not be late now?"

When Matt didn't answer, she turned to her left and to her right but soon discovered that she was alone. "Matt?" she called out into the darkness. "Matt! Where are you?"

Suddenly, Mavis saw a movement to her left. Squinting in the darkness, she saw that it was Matt, struggling in her direction in the bite suit. He was walking jerkily, with a major stagger to and fro with each step he took. He also wore a black motorcycle helmet with a dark visor, so his head was protected, though she couldn't see his face. Swinging from one hand was the leather-strapped, concrete-filled fish bat. As Matt walked, the bat swung grotesquely to and fro, hitting him in the thigh every now and again.

She heard the noise of laughter coming from the direction of the woods; it was the voice of Shanice Hall.

"Mavis!" Shanice's voice had a sing-song quality to it that was silly while it was threatening, and it instilled fear deep inside of Mavis. She froze, staring in the direction of the woods and trying to block out the sound of Matt as he struggled in the bite suit.

After a little while, the shadow of her enemy appeared, but the girl wasn't alone. As she left the woods and started down the grassy hill toward the lot Mavis was in, Mavis saw that she had not one, but two people with her. One was obviously a man, but he was stocky and had short-cropped hair. He didn't look anything like the description of Gunnar that Kim had given them: slender with a long, dark ponytail. That didn't matter half as much as the other person with her: a curvy girl with long waves of hair that hung past her shoulders.

Kim Coleman.

The three of them staggered and lurched in Mavis' direction. She could hear Shanice's laughter, but as they neared she could also hear gurgling sounds and the sound of wet lips smacking together. Her stomach turned, and fear filled her heart.

"Matt, hurry up!" she yelled. "They're here, and she has Kim and Shawn with her! Hurry!"

She turned to the right to see how far away Matt was, and much to her surprise he was standing right next to her. "This is no time for games, Matthew! Look! Here they come!"

He didn't answer her, though; he simply continued to look at her without making a noise of any kind. Finally, she had enough of his games and reached out to touch the helmet, flipping the visor upward to expose his face. There, behind the visor, was Matt Morgan, but he was no longer the Matt that Mavis had come to know and love. He was pasty white, with dark circles under his eyes and large chunks of skin missing from his graying face. He smiled at her, and a large centipede, along with several spiders and maggots crawled from his mouth. Mavis couldn't move; the fear of the situation took over completely, rendering her powerless.

"What did you think was going to happen, Mavis?" he asked her in a voice that sounded like he was gargling gravel. "Didn't you know? This was the plan all along! The world will be like us! The world will be like us! The entire world!"

She stood there, overcome with shock and disbelief. With her eyes fixed on her beloved Matthew, who was obviously one of the undead now, and looking at her like she was a steak, she realized that she couldn't move. Oh, she thought, I'm petrified with fear! I can't move a muscle!"

Just as she tried to look over her shoulder, she felt the hands all over her. Shanice's hands, Kim's hands, and Shawn's hands were grabbing, ripping, and pulling her to the dirty, rocky ground. Before long she was lying on her back, her arms and legs being held down by the three while Matt stood over her in that silly bite suit. He was looking down at her, his smile wide. A single tooth fell out of its socket and bounced off her forehead.

"Time to put you out of your flesh-eating misery, Mavis," he growled. "Time to send you to where you came from, so we can make the world our own. Are you ready?"

Mavis began to shake her head crazily, back and forth, until she could almost feel her dead, rotting brain rattling against her skull inside. "No!" she screamed. "This isn't right! This isn't the way it's supposed to be!"

But Kim, Shawn, and Shanice had a good hold on her, and she couldn't move or even fight back very well. As she struggled, she saw Matt's smile grow. He began to draw back his arm, the fish bat gripped firmly in his hand, and right then Mavis realized what was going to happen: he was going to bash her brains in. He was going to put an end to Mavis.

"No, Matthew! No! It's me, Matt! Mavis!"

But he didn't hear her. He swung, hard, bringing the bat down toward her with great strength.

The last thing she saw were the words "Bass Basher" right before the bat hit her forehead...

CHAPTER 29

"Mavis! Mavis, wake up! You're having a nightmare!"

Matt was sitting on the edge of her bed, a firm grip on her shoulders as he gently shook her in his attempt to bring her back to reality. It didn't take her long to snap out of it; with a rapid shake of her head and a good look around her room, she was back to reality. Matt sat patiently, watching her and waiting for her to speak.

"It was just a bad dream," she muttered after a moment, swinging her feet around to the floor. The stress from all of this is just taking its toll, that's all."

Mavis glanced at her bedside clock; it was nearly five-fifteen. "Mom will be calling for dinner soon."

"That's why I came in to wake you," Matt said, taking her by the hand. "She already did. I figured we could make our appearance with them, then you could come in here and eat something from the cooler. Soon enough it will be eleven, and I think it's smart to be at the park around 10:30."

With a nod, Mavis replied, "Give me a minute, Matt, would you? I need to give Kim a quick call, okay?"

"Sure thing."

Matt left, and Mavis waited until she heard his footsteps move away in the hall before picking up her cell and dialing her best friend. The phone rang four times before the girl picked it up. Mavis had started to wonder if she was going to answer at all.

"Hey, Kim," she greeted gently, almost sadly. "I didn't interrupt your dinner, did I?"

After a pause, Kim replied, "No. I'm eating out with Shawn before the movie. He's picking me up in a few minutes. Listen, Mavis, I'm sorry I got so hot under the collar earlier. It's just that Shanice seemed so sincere and all; I guess I just wanted to give her the benefit of the doubt, you know? But deep inside I guess I know that you're right."

"That's why I called, Kim. I just wanted you to be careful. If you happen to see her, be sure you only talk to her around other people." Mavis paused and closed her eyes, saying a silent prayer for her best friend and Shawn. "I talked to her after we talked and she seemed entertained or something by the fact that you took the tickets, so please, just promise me that you'll be careful, okay?"

"I promise, Mav."

Intentionally, Mavis changed her tone to one of cheer. "So, you're going to have to give me a full report on the movie. I hear it's supposed to be a real hoot."

"Promise. You'll get the full rundown."

With that, they disconnected the call, and Mavis made her way to the bathroom to wash up for supper. Her parents would be waiting for her at the table, along with Matt. It wouldn't do for things to seem off, not tonight. She needed her parents to go to bed just like always, without suspicion and ready for a good night's sleep.

"Well, it's about time," Todd teased when she entered the dining room. "I can hardly believe you'd be late for steak and potatoes, Mav."

Mavis gave a laugh that was weak, but convincing. "I guess that I was sleeping a bit harder than I would have liked. Sorry for making all of you wait."

"No problem, Dear." Jane spread her napkin out over her lap. "But now that you're here let's dig in, shall we? Your dad slaved long and hard over the grill."

Todd, Jane, and Matt hit the food as if it were the first meal they'd had in a long time, but Mavis started eating slowly at first. It wasn't until she noticed the looks of doubt she was getting from her parents, and the kick that Matt gave her under the table, that she started eating with a bit more gusto. The steak was done perfectly, but to her, it was like tasteless rubber. She forced a moan of "yumminess" with each bite until her parents were satisfied that she was enjoying the food. In reality, she was practically choking it down.

The conversation that night was light, and everyone seemed to avoid the topic that seemed to be filling each and every household: the cannibal murders. Her parents always had a way of avoiding stressful conversation at mealtimes, especially when it came to murder and mayhem. Lately, it seemed that was all anyone discussed or worried about, and all of them wanted to put it out of their minds and away from the table that night. They ate, talked about Todd's job, the fact that the flower season was wrapping up, a funny stunt Grandma Cabot pulled at the bingo hall, and the kids' studies. The conversation was light and cheerful, at least, as cheerful as it could be. But unbeknownst to Mavis' parents, both she and Matt were on the edge of their seats. The front they put on was perfect, however, and neither adult showed suspicion in any way.

They finished eating around six, and Mavis helped clean up the supper mess while Matt and Todd watched the evening news. Afterward, they all sat down and played a game, but Mavis' heart wasn't in it. All she could think about was Kim and Shawn, and the fact that they were going to a show that Shanice Hall had provided the tickets for. Her mind kept whirling around the situation, and her upset stomach told her that something was indeed wrong, but no matter how hard she tried, she just couldn't put a finger on it.

The time crept by in a dreadfully slow manner, but soon Jane and Todd were ready to turn in: it was nearly ten. Todd liked to watch the world news in his room, and both of them typically fell asleep during the broadcast. Mavis and Matt hung out in her bedroom, pretending to play a second round, but they were really getting ready. They planned to leave around 10:30 since her parents had turned in later than she expected. No matter what, they would be on time.

Finally, at 10:25, Mavis raised the volume slightly on a music video channel, but only after pressing her ear to the wall and confirming the light snores coming from her parents' room. They climbed out her bedroom window and ran for the car; they planned to take her convertible since Matt's car was a bit too loud for such sneakiness.

His bite suit and bat were already in the backseat. Mavis would drive while he suited up, and he would be ready by the time they got to Donnelly Park. The park would have closed at ten, but they would enter the perimeter the back way, which was closer to the meeting place than the main entrance, and out of sight of the general public. As she drove in silence, she wondered if Shanice would come by car, or if she and her lackey would be on foot. It didn't matter, she realized after a moment; the most important thing wasn't how they got there, only that they arrived.

Before she knew it, they were sitting at the back entrance, the car idling quietly. She turned to Matt in the back seat, and a huge smile broke out on her face. He looked like the big puffy guy from the tire commercials.

"You should see yourself," she giggled. "You should be safe from bites, but if you fall down, you might not be able to get back up."

"Ha, ha, ha," he retorted sarcastically. "Don't you worry; I've been practicing, and I believe in myself. Now, we're going to drive in, and I want you to park right where they can see us. We don't know how they're getting here, but it doesn't matter. I have a feeling they'll be on time, and we'll see them soon enough."

Mavis didn't respond, she simply began to pull into

Donnelly slowly, navigating the narrow car paths carefully and with little to no acceleration. The last thing she wanted was to draw attention of any kind. She just wanted to get there and get all of this madness over with. No matter how it ended up, at least, it would be over.

At last, they arrived at the big tree, which in Mavis' mind was the landmark she was looking for. She parked next to it and immediately turned off the engine. There was a single light illuminating the area, and it didn't provide light for any distance at all.

"10:40," Matt said quietly. "Time to get out."

Mavis hopped out of the car, while Matt had a bit more of a struggle, but soon they were standing next to the car, both of them set to "super vigilance." They looked around in silence, looking for any sign of Shanice and her pal.

Time ticked by so slowly that it didn't seem to be passing at all. But like time does, it did pass, and before she knew it, it was nearly five minutes to eleven. Her hands were beginning to tremble, and she felt herself tensing up.

"Mavis, look."

She turned and glanced behind her, in the direction which they had come into the park, and sure enough, there was a van coming in their direction. The presence of the van threw her off, making her think that some stranger was going to mess things up for them. But when it pulled into a spot just near them, she got a glance at the passenger: a smiling, excited Shanice. The car was being driven by someone with a ponytail: Gunnar. She also thought she could hear a couple of thumps and other odd sounds coming from the vehicle, but her mind and nerves would not allow her to pay attention.

The van stopped and shut off, and Shanice and Gunnar got out. Soon, both of them were standing by the van, facing Mavis and Matt. Gunnar still wore a patch over his eye, but he didn't seem to mind. He was looking at them both as if he couldn't wait to put them out of their misery.

"Hello, Mavis," Shanice sneered. "At last, we come face to face, and we get to see who the best zombie is."

Neither Mavis nor Matt replied; they simply stood and listened.

"What is this Halloween costume your friend is wearing?" Shanice took a step forward and inhaled deeply. "Oh! It's one of those dog suits! That's okay; it won't stop me. I intend to make Matthew Morgan into my dinner. Oh, I almost forgot... we have a surprise for you."

Shanice turned to Gunnar and gave him a nod. With half a smile, he went to the back of the van and opened the rear doors. Two people with bags over their heads tumbled out, cursing and flailing. Gunnar pulled the bags off, and that was when Mavis realized the truth.

Shanice had, indeed, brought Kim and Shawn; she intended to make game of all of them.

R.W.K. Clark

CHAPTER 30

As soon as Mavis saw Kim and Shawn, she froze. She had known this was going to happen, yet she did nothing about it. Wanting to cry and scream, she pushed all of her emotions down as far as she could and glared at Shanice.

"You are the bottom of the barrel when it comes to human beings," she sneered at Shanice. "You're nothing more than a bully."

Shanice laughed hard. "I've known that since the day I was born, and I'm happy this way."

Mavis began to walk back and forth, her eyes focused on Kim and Shawn, who Gunnar had now pushed to the ground. Their hands were bound behind their backs, and they were gagged with bandannas. Kim was crying, mascara streaking down her face, while Shawn struggled angrily against the ropes, to no avail.

"So, it is going to be you and Gunnar, I will take dog boy." Shanice laughed. "I guess since I cheated, it's only fair to let you decide when we begin."

That was all it took for Mavis. She turned to Gunnar and let out a roar, then rushed at him with all her might. Her body hit his like a ton of bricks, knocking him into the side of the van hard. He slid down and landed on the ground next to Mavis' friends, looked up at her, and smiled.

"She likes to play rough, Shanice," Gunnar said as he got to his feet. "You didn't tell me that; this will be fun. And when I beat you, Mavis, I get Kim as my reward."

But Shanice didn't answer; she and Matt were already going at it full force, with all they had. They were on the ground, rolling and struggling. The fish bat dangled uselessly from his wrist, but the rest of him was sufficiently covered to protect him. When Mavis saw that Shanice was having a hard time with him, she turned her full attention to Gunnar, who was swinging at her with his arms like a windmill gone bad.

Kim was crying and trying to scream while Shawn was focusing on getting the ropes off, but he was making no progress. Mavis was giving Gunnar her best, smashing her fist into his head as hard as she could. At first, none of her blows seemed to be having an effect, but then she reared back and gave him a really good one, and he was stunned hard.

The man lay on the ground, grunting and shaking his head slightly as if trying to clear it. His eyes were crossed, and Mavis knew she had done some kind of damage, but she wasn't sure how much. Right then, she decided to take the opportunity to try and free Shawn… he was their best hope for assistance at that point.

She tugged and pulled at the ropes, glancing back at Gunnar now and then. That was when she noticed that she had actually caved his head in slightly on one side, and she knew then that he was down for the count. Soon, Mavis had Shawn free, so she rushed over to help Matt, who was lying on his back on the ground, kicking and flailing, like a bug which was knocked off balance. Shanice stood over him, smiling. She was preparing to take off his helmet and take a healthy bite, and Mavis knew it.

Mavis bum rushed Shanice, and the girl went flying, hitting the ground hard. But she simply laughed and hopped back to her feet as if she were on a spring. Glancing over her shoulder, she could see Kim had gotten to her feet and was running off as quickly as she could.

"Run, Kim! Go!"

Her friend listened to her wholeheartedly this time, not doubting her at all. But then she saw that somehow Gunnar had come to his senses. He was getting to his feet, and his eyes were on Kim. Matt was up now too, and both of them ran to Gunnar. It was then that Matt took the fish bat to Gunnar's head, beating him over and over until his brains oozed out and there was nothing left of him but a heap of dead, decaying flesh without an ounce of life left in it.

One down, one to go.

But then the worst happened. While Mavis and Matt had been beating on Gunnar, Shawn had decided somewhere in his dim mind that he could take Shanice. It was the biggest mistake he would ever make in his life.

Shanice and Shawn were a good thirty feet from them, in the grass. He was trying to fight her off, but her zombie strength was too much for him. While he punched her in the stomach and torso, she laughed at him, standing there and taking it. He had no idea he should be aiming for her head, and that lack of knowledge would prove to be his undoing.

He gave her one last solid hit to the chest, even caving it in a bit, and Shanice began to laugh harder than ever. Kim was nowhere to be seen, but Mavis could hear her, sobbing uncontrollably with fear, in the bushes about ten feet away. She turned back to Shawn and Shanice just as Matt was running for them, his fish bat in the air.

It was too late.

Shanice had sunk her teeth into his neck and tore his jugular away from his body, ripping it out in a long stringer that was followed by a spurt of blood that would rival a fountain. Matt and Mavis both froze, horrified. There was no saving Shawn Maher now.

Shawn Maher was, indeed, dinner for Shanice Hall.

Behind them, they could hear Kim scream through her gag.

Mavis ran full force at Shanice, who pulled the dead football player into the back of the van, then slammed the doors.

"Well," she said cheerfully out the driver window as she started the engine, "I had a feeling it would end up like this, or at least in a similar way. But I have my meal. Gunnar was just a pawn, just like everyone I have ever known… or ever will know."

She floored the gas and took off through the rear entrance of the park. As the sound of her engine faded, all that could be heard was the sound of Kim's hysterical tears. While Matt struggled to free himself of the bite suit, Mavis ran to find her friend.

Kim was still bound and gagged, covered in dirt and crying. She had seen everything, and she was hysterical. Mavis grabbed the gag and pulled it free quickly, then helped Kim to her feet. Kim fell into her arms, sobbing.

"Go… go after them! She has him! She has Shawn! She's going to eat him!"

Mavis held her friend tightly. "Shhh," she whispered into her ear. "Cry it out. Let it out."

"Why aren't you going after her, Mavis? Why?"

Mavis held her away and looked seriously into her eyes. "It's too late, Kim. He was already gone."

Immediately, Kim's eyes rolled back into her head, and she fainted dead away.

Matt helped Mavis put Kim into the backseat of the car once they untied her. He then took the bite suit, helmet, and fish bat and loaded it into the trunk. The pair then got into the car, this time with Matt driving, and made their way out of the park and headed to Mavis' house. They would take Kim in, and when she woke, freaking out, they would do all they could to calm her. But Mavis knew that the only way to make this right would be to go to the cops; Kim would insist, she was sure.

On the way home, they drove by Shanice's loft, but

there were no lights on in the unit.

"I don't think she's going to be coming back here at all," Matt said. "I think she's going to take things to the next level, whatever that is. I don't even know if that involves you."

Mavis just stared at the building, anger boiling inside of her. "Oh, it involves me. And if it doesn't, it will. I'll make sure of it."

After a short time, they headed back for the Harvey house, where the rest of the night was spent trying to calm a now conscious Kim while explaining what had happened to Todd and Jane. They told the parents everything, only leaving out the fact that Mavis was a zombie. They told them that Shanice had been the murderer all along and that her goal had been revenge on Mavis. Surprisingly, Kim went along with it all, even in her hysterics.

Jane called Kim's mother, who gave her permission to give Kim a mild sedative. Once Kim was calm and waiting for her parents, Jane and Todd gave the kids a few minutes alone. Mavis wasn't sure what Kim would say, but she waited patiently.

Finally, she spoke. "If I had just listened, none of this would have happened."

Mavis just shook her head. "You couldn't have known."

Kim ignored her. "If we call the cops, we'll never get her ourselves."

"Yes, we will," Matt said. "She won't get busted by the cops. She has too much money; she can leave the country if she wants. But I don't think she will. I think she'll change her name and stick close by. This was never about Shawn, or you, or me. It's about Mavis. Besides, we've already told Jane, and the cops will be here any minute. You just listen to us, and I promise, we're going to get this crazy psycho, Kim. I promise."

Kim's parents showed up, as did the cops. The kids told the police that Matt and Mavis got a call saying that Shanice Hall had Kim and Shawn, and if they wanted them back they had to meet her at the park. They did, and that was when Shanice and her pal Gunnar took Shawn hostage, but not before biting him. They told police the young man was bleeding profusely from the neck when they took him.

They also made sure that police understood that this was all about revenge for the attack last year that Shanice was arrested for. They told them where her loft was, and that she was using her mother's identity. The police were there until nearly four in the morning, though they let Kim go home with her parents around 1:30 since the sedative had rendered her worthless.

By the time the cops left, the sun was rising, and the birds were beginning to chirp. Matt and Mavis sat with cups of coffee, listening to Todd and Jane lecture them to no end about what they had done. They should never have left alone; they should have called the police immediately.

But what was done was done.

Now it was Sunday. By ten in the morning, they received a call from police confirming that Shanice's apartment had been completely cleaned out and all but deserted. The girl had left no sign of where she may have gone, but the cops warned them all to watch their backs. They suspected she wasn't finished with her revenge, considering all the lengths she had gone to in this situation.

Mavis and Matt both knew they were right. It wasn't a matter of whether or not she would attack again... it was a matter of when.

CHAPTER 31

Shanice Hall sat on her plush towel in the sand at a beach resort and casino. It was warm here, which she liked because she was cold all the time anymore. With her sunglasses over her eyes, she looked directly into the sun and thought about Mavis; the thought made her smile.

Technically, her enemy had gotten the best of her; nothing had turned out the way she intended or planned, but that didn't matter. She had gotten away, and she had done so with a big load of food in that football player, Shawn. But if things had gone perfectly, all of them would have been dead except, of course, for her and Gunnar. She had underestimated Mavis, a mistake she wouldn't make again.

It certainly didn't help that the girl was so straight-laced. Had she an ounce of evil in her, Shanice would have come out ahead. Oh, well, she thought as she stretched out in a leisurely fashion. There was always next time… and there would be a next time.

"Your drink, Madam?"

Shanice turned to see a blond pool boy with big muscles holding out a pink cocktail with a turquoise umbrella. He was smiling down at her, his blue eyes shining. She always had a thing for blue-eyed young men.

"Thank you," she replied, taking the drink. "Tell me, do you have free time in the evening? Do they let you date the patrons?"

His smile grew. "I can date whoever I want, beautiful, and hello, my name is Brad."

"Shanice," she grinned. "Well, that's a surprise," she replied. "Usually a place like this doesn't want their help to mix business with pleasure. Not to mention that I find it hard to believe that you don't have a girlfriend that would make it difficult for us to have a good time."

The young man chuckled. "Well, here I think they see it more as a strategic business move than a threat. As for girlfriends, well, I just don't have the time. Why? Did you have something in mind?"

"I don't know, but I think you are one gorgeous hunk of meat," she purred.

The blond knelt down beside her and leaned in. "You're pretty outstanding yourself."

Shanice looked him over good through her shades; he was muscle all over, and he didn't seem all too stupid, either.

He nodded dumbly but continued to smile, flashing his pearly whites dynamically. Shanice thought that maybe he depended too much on those perfect teeth of his, and those perfect good looks. Well, he wouldn't have to depend on anything for too long, because she had plans for him.

"So, do you want to hook up?" she asked lightly.

He nodded quickly. "Shanice, I'm sure with you, whatever it is won't be boring."

She took a long sip of her drink, giggled entertainingly, and turned back to him. "Well Brad, I was wondering how you might feel about me having you for dinner…"

ENTREATY

This book was made possible by reviews from readers like you. Reviews fuel my creativity. If you enjoyed this novel, I implore you to please write a review and share your experience on the retailer's website. The livelihood for authors is entirely dependent on reviews, and I must say, it is the largest obstacle as a struggling author that I have encountered. Please tell a friend, tell a loved one about this read. With your help, I will be one step closer to overcoming this obstacle. In return, I thank you from the bottom of my heart, and sincerely appreciate your time and effort.

Humbled, with gratitude,

R.W.K. Clark

ABOUT THE AUTHOR

I am a father of two beautiful children, Jon and Kim. They are my motivating forces; they are the lighthouse in this vast ocean. In my life, they are the air that I breathe; they are the oasis in this desert of uncertainty. They are my greatest joy in life and my number one priority. I have a long list of hobbies, and I attribute that to my lust for life! I like to surround myself with positive people, who share the same interests. Family values, the arts, outdoors, nature, and travel are tops on my list. I embrace attending cultural and artistic events because I believe dramatic self-expression is the window to the soul. I wear my heart on my sleeve, and I still believe in chivalry, and I always treat people the way I want to be treated.

www.rwkclark.com